"What if today 〰 P9-BZI-433
Lexi asked.

As the tornado surged outside, she looked up at him and wondered why she had let him go so easily. The words were definitely more maudlin than she'd intended.

"At least we're together," he said.

"Together?" She shook her head. She knew without a doubt that she wasn't over her husband. He whispered that he sometimes felt the same way and she smiled, even though she knew it wasn't real. This wasn't real.

But his arms around her were real. This was what happened when two people were afraid and they didn't know if they would have a tomorrow. And if they did survive, they'd go back to living separate lives, careful to never really look at one another. But for this moment, with their lives hanging in the balance, she chose to not think about it, about tomorrow, and about losing him all over again.

**After the Storm:**
**A Kansas community unites to rebuild**

**Books by Brenda Minton**

Love Inspired

*Trusting Him*
*His Little Cowgirl*
*A Cowboy's Heart*
*The Cowboy Next Door*
*Rekindled Hearts*

## *BRENDA MINTON*

started creating stories to entertain herself during hour-long rides on the school bus. In high school she wrote romance novels to entertain her friends. The dream grew and so did her aspirations to become an author. She started with notebooks, handwritten manuscripts and characters that refused to go away until their stories were told. Eventually she put away the pen and paper and got down to business with the computer. The journey took a few years, with some encouragement and rejection along the way—as well as a lot of stubbornness on her part. In 2006, her dream to write for Steeple Hill Books came true.

Brenda lives in the rural Ozarks with her husband, three kids and an abundance of cats and dogs. She enjoys a chaotic life that she wouldn't trade for anything—except, on occasion, a beach house in Texas. You can stop by and visit at her Web site, www.brendaminton.net.

# Rekindled Hearts
## Brenda Minton

Steeple
Hill®

Published by Steeple Hill Books™

Special thanks and acknowledgment to Brenda Minton for her contribution to the After the Storm miniseries.

STEEPLE HILL BOOKS

Steeple
Hill®

Recycling programs
for this product may
not exist in your area.

ISBN-13: 978-0-373-81426-8

REKINDLED HEARTS

www.SteepleHill.com

**Printed in U.S.A.**

Then maidens will dance and be glad,
young men and old as well.
I will turn their mourning into gladness;
I will give them comfort and joy instead of sorrow.
—*Jeremiah* 31:13

I would like to dedicate this book to my family, for understanding deadlines. To the editors at Love Inspired, for giving me the opportunity to do this story. To my agent, Janet Benrey, for being the best. To survivors everywhere.

# Prologue

*July 10*

The patrol car cruised Main Street of High Plains. There was no breeze, just July heat and heavy humidity. A glance out the open car window confirmed what Police Chief Colt Ridgeway already knew. It was anything but a normal day. The air was too still and the sky had that funky green tint that set a guy's nerves on edge and raised the hair on his arms.

Foreboding, there was a definite sense of foreboding with the town streets nearly empty at four in the afternoon and the leaves on the trees turned bottom up in advance of the rains that were coming.

Colt had been sitting in his car on a road at the edge of town, storm spotting. Now he headed for the police department connected to the fire station.

Two of his officers were still posted on side roads, as were several volunteer firemen. From the looks of things, High Plains, Kansas, was in big trouble. The southern horizon was dark and the clouds rolled. A definite wall cloud had formed and he could see the rotation, even at this distance.

His scanner blasted the information about the latest warning and the tornado siren connected to the town hall went off. The sound blared loud and then soft as it rotated on the pole. Colt hit his siren and lights.

A dozen or more times a year they went through this same scenario, cruising the streets and neighborhoods of High Plains to warn the residents that a tornado had been spotted. If people couldn't hear the tornado siren, he wanted them to hear the siren on his car.

His radio crackled and the voice of one of his officers, breaking up but discernible, blasted his ear. Colt lowered the volume.

"Go ahead, Bud."

"Chief, it's on the ground, ten or fifteen miles out of town." A muttered comment from Bud.

"Take shelter, Bud."

"God save…" The deputy's voice faded.

"Bud?" No answer. Colt had to hope it was just interference. He really had to hope, because the kid was young and just out of the police academy.

Colt wouldn't lose an officer. He shook his head, remembering the younger cop's shortened sentence. *God save us.*

God wasn't going to save them. Colt could have told the younger officer that he'd prayed more than once in his life, and he wasn't sure God was listening.

Maybe this time?

Until God proved Himself, Colt would have to do the saving. The people of High Plains had entrusted him with that duty. He drove through a quiet neighborhood, his siren blaring, and headed back to Main Street. The wind picked up and he could smell rain. He could see the dark band of precipitation heading their way.

And above the wind and thunder, he could hear something else. A dog howling. Or he thought it was a dog.

He tried to listen, leaning out a little, but the wind was whipping and he had to put up his window. His radio crackled again. Bud's voice broke, crackled and then dissolved into nothing.

The siren on his car blended in with the sound of the storm, the tornado siren and the barking dog. Colt glanced to his left, to the street that led to Lexi's house. He swallowed the lump that rose in his throat, the lump that just thinking about her caused. And then it was fear, because he had to work and couldn't keep her safe.

Besides that, she wasn't his wife anymore. He had to let her go.

He *had* let go. Of course he had. Because he had to let her find happiness, a life that included her dream of having a family.

They had both moved on. He had even dated a little.

A newspaper blew, catching on the wipers of the car. Rain fell in sheets so heavy it was hard to see the street. Trees along the meandering High Plains River, barely a creek most of the time, were circling and bending as the wind picked up.

Ahead of him, just a few blocks away, Tommy Jacobs was riding a bike in the rain that was becoming a downpour. Who let a six-year-old out in weather like this? No way had Beth and Brandon Otis, the boy's foster parents, let him out to play. That was just Tommy, always sneaking off with that old dog of his. He had probably been in the middle of doing what he loved most, annoying Gregory Garrison, when the storm hit. And now he was too far from home to make it safely.

Colt did a quick check of the horizon, confirming his worst suspicions. The black, swirling clouds were gaining ground, gaining in size. He could see the swirling debris. Trees in the park were leaning with the force of winds that pushed ahead of the storm.

Tommy was scrunched down on his bike and probably pretty scared and miserable. Colt hit the gas, because he had to get that kid.

Charlie, the dog, looked to be barking at the tires of Tommy's bike. The dog wanted to go home, too. Colt hit the gas as his stomach tightened. The sky was darker. The wind blowing harder. The kid was leaning on his bike.

Colt hit the siren twice, hoping the boy would pay attention. The door to Gregory Garrison's office opened, and the businessman grabbed the kid off the bike and hauled him inside just as it was starting to hail. Colt waved, breathing a sigh of relief. The kid would be safe with Greg and his assistant, Maya Logan.

The rest of the town was deserted. People had heeded the warning and taken shelter. He glanced toward the day care. The kids would be safe there. He didn't see anyone outside. The only movement was on the city green, next to the gazebo. Colt's dog, Chico. The stupid chocolate lab was barking at the storm as wind blew and a few small trees toppled.

Even the mildest storm, if it included thunder and lightning, caused the dog to lose it. Chico had one spot in the fence that he could dig his way out of. Since the dog couldn't get inside Colt's house, he was probably heading for Lexi's.

The roar of the wind increased. He couldn't see the funnel from where he was, but he knew that it was out there. And he had no idea where it was heading.

"God save us."

He repeated Bud's words, because he knew he couldn't save himself. Dust filled the car, filling his nostrils with the scent of destruction and earth. His heart pounded and the sound roared in his ears.

He wasn't ready to die.

He wasn't going to let his dog die. He jumped out of the car and ran toward the dog, shouting his name, knowing the animal couldn't hear above the roaring wind. A piece of metal flew through the air, bouncing off the ground and then into the air again.

Colt yelled at the dog. Chico turned and as he did, the metal hit his side and the dog fell.

The pull of the storm made it hard to move, hard to breathe. Colt leaned, pushing himself forward. When he reached the dog, he kneeled, breathing deep for a moment, giving his heart a second to slow its pounding rhythm, letting his lungs refill.

The rain had slowed, still heavy, but not pounding. Debris floated in the wind and fluttered to the ground. They were in serious trouble.

The pieces of siding and insulation had to come from homes in the outlying areas. To the south he could see the form of a dark wall cloud. The air had stilled, but the storms weren't over.

He had to get hold of Bud, or one of the storm spotters, to see what was happening outside of town. And they would have to notify the county officers to make sure they were in the area.

He keyed his mic. Nothing. He pulled his cell phone out, hoping for a signal. He still had one. That meant they still had towers standing. When Bud answered, he could hear the younger cop's fear in his shaking voice. Colt wondered if he sounded the same.

"Bud, what's it look like out there?"

"Bad, Chief. I saw a county deputy. He said there's a tornado forming. It was on the ground for a while, and went back up, but it's still there. I can see the rotation."

"Okay, make sure the county emergency management has been contacted. You might want to contact the hospital and some of the other communities around here. If they haven't been hit, we're going to need their help." He held a handkerchief to the wound on his dog's side.

"Sure thing. Oh man, it's on the ground again."

"Bud, take shelter somewhere. When it's over, we'll do house-by-house searches. But stay safe."

"Got it. You, too, 'cause it's heading that way."

Colt slid his phone back into his pocket and turned his attention back to the dog. "I've got to get you to Lexi's before this hits."

The wind picked up, blowing across the lawn. Colt glanced toward the High Plains Community Church. He could make it there. But two blocks away was Lexi's house and veterinary clinic. Was she there, or out on a call?

He had to make sure she was okay. "Come on, Chico."

But the dog wasn't moving. "Buddy, don't ask me to do this."

The dog raised his head and looked up at him.

"Come on." Colt scooped the sixty-pound dog into his arms. More blood oozed from the cut.

As the storm rolled toward them he ran across Main Street and down the road toward Lexi's, and safety. And if she wasn't home? He didn't want to think of her out on the road, tending sick cows in the middle of a tornado.

Lexi stood in the entryway of her house, knowing that she shouldn't be there. She should be back in the basement, where she'd gone after she had first heard the siren. But her heart wouldn't let her go back, not until she knew if Colt was safe. She'd watched his car pass earlier.

She knew he would risk his life to save everyone else. He was all about saving other people. If only he had put that same care into their marriage.

He said he had divorced her to save her from heartache.

Whatever.

She knew that he had divorced her to save himself. He didn't want to live his life worrying about her, worrying about what would happen to her if something happened to him. He had divorced her because he hadn't been able to deal with the death of Gavin Jones, a deputy that Colt hadn't been able to reach in time to save.

As mad as he made her, Lexi's heart still ached when she thought of Colt, of loving him and losing him. She closed her eyes and leaned against the cool glass of the window.

She prayed he would be safe. This felt too much like their marriage, when she had prayed every night that he would come home safe. And one night, a few months after Gavin's death, he hadn't called to let her know he would be late.

He had found her on the couch, crying, afraid something had happened to him. That night had been the final straw for them both.

Now he was out there again. And she was afraid. Again.

It had to be bad. Debris littered her yard. Her

power was out and the house was silent. No news on the radio, no hum of the fridge. Silence, other than the howl of the wind picking up again, and rain pelting the windows and metal roof.

"Please, God, keep him safe. Keep our town safe." The wood door shuddered and heaved as the wind ripped across the Kansas plains.

She should go to the basement.

As she turned away from the door it blew open. And there he was, bloody and heaving as he carried their dog into the house. His dog. Chico had been hers, but after the divorce, he picked Colt.

The dog had broken her heart, too. Each time she'd bring him back home, the dog would run back to Colt's.

"Colt." She froze for a second and then came to life again, because the house shuddered and the wind outside had changed. It wasn't blowing straight at the house the way it had. Windows on all sides seemed to be taking a beating from wind and rain, leaves sticking to the glass.

"Get to the basement." Colt's blond hair was rain-soaked and plastered to his head. A streak of blood marked his cheek. *"Lexi, go!"*

She ran down the hall to the door that led to the basement. She opened it and motioned him down. Before she could go, she needed supplies. She needed something for him, or the dog, whichever one was injured. Her clinic was on the lot next to the house. She couldn't make it over there, not in this storm.

"Lexi, down here now."

"I'm coming."

She grabbed a few things from the kitchen counter and ran down the stairs, slamming the door behind her. She held the rail and took careful steps in the darkened basement, glad to see a sliver of light from the small window and then the bright beam of a flashlight Colt had found.

"I'm here, in the corner." Colt's voice, soft and firm. He never panicked.

Lexi bit down on her lip, listening to the crash and splinter of trees and the wind slamming her house. Her heart pounded painfully in her chest and she didn't want this to happen, not this, not now.

Not when she was finally starting to get it together again. Total destruction was a perfect marriage crumbling into a nightmare of silence and loneliness. This nightmare she couldn't take, not the town crumbling around her.

What was God thinking? Did He know she had been at the end of her faith rope and she was just beginning to climb back up?

Chico was on the table she used for folding laundry. His side was gashed open and blood oozed from the wound. She glanced up, making eye contact with blue eyes that had once danced with laughter.

When had Colt stopped laughing?

She searched through the supplies she'd grabbed, and Colt moved closer. He grimaced and held his left arm close to his chest with his right hand.

"Are you okay?"

He smiled, as if it didn't matter. "Take care of Chico, I'm fine."

A loud crash sounded above them and then shattering glass. She shuddered and paused, waiting to see if everything would collapse in on them. When the world calmed for a minute, she looked at Colt again, at the arm he held to his side.

"Of course you're fine." She touched his arm and he flinched. His face was bruised, as well. "What happened out there?"

Tight lines of pain around his mouth. "We're taking a direct hit. I need to make sure the two of you are okay and get back out there."

"Not until I make sure you're okay. You look like you were in a car accident."

"It was nothing like that. A tree limb hit my arm." He wouldn't tell her more. She knew he didn't want her to picture what had happened out there. What was still happening. But she could hear it.

She cut into a sheet and ripped a strip of cloth away. She tied the ends and handed it to him. She wouldn't put it around his neck. She couldn't do that. Tight lips formed a smile and he slipped the makeshift sling over his neck.

A huge crash above them. Lexi jumped and shuddered, tingles sliding up her arms and through her scalp. She closed her eyes and waited.

"Lexi, it's okay." Colt's voice, steady and calm.

She opened her eyes, and he was watching her.

"Of course it is." She tried to smile but she couldn't, not with the storm raging outside her home and fear tangling with adrenaline inside her heart. "The town falling in around us is okay."

"We're safe."

She nodded, not really believing it. She'd watched the news all morning, watching national coverage of storms ripping across Kansas, taking lives, taking homes and dreams. She had prayed that it would stop, that it would turn away from them.

Chico whimpered and raised his head to look at her, his sad eyes pleading. Lexi smoothed his brown coat and examined the cut. "I'm going to give him a shot and then clean this out and sew it up."

"Is he going to be okay?" Little-boy eyes in the face of a man. She nodded and looked away.

Last week she'd gone out with a farmer from a neighboring town. He had two children and dimples. She had liked him. He wasn't complicated. He wasn't Colt.

"He'll be fine. But he's losing a lot of blood, and I don't have an IV down here."

"I'll run upstairs and get one."

"You can't run upstairs. It's too dangerous and you don't know what I need." Everything she said seemed to have a double meaning. She looked away from him.

"This isn't the first animal I've tended to with you, Lexi. I know what you need. I'll get it, and then if it's clear enough, I need to get back to town. I need to make sure people are safe."

"The storm."

"Don't worry." He winked, as if it really was okay.

"I don't want to be alone." Honesty. She bit down on her bottom lip as he looked away. "I don't want to die down here alone."

"You're safe, Lex. We're both safe."

She wanted to hold on to him, refusing to let him leave her alone. Instead she nodded, and she let him go. "Get what I need while I close this wound."

And he was gone.

She listened to him upstairs, slamming cabinets. The wind pounded the house and something upstairs crashed. She shuddered because she knew it wasn't Colt. He was tall and muscular, but not clumsy.

She sutured Chico's wound, talking quietly to her dog, and praying they'd all survive this. Quiet tears slipped down her cheeks and she couldn't brush them away with gloved hands. She used her arm.

But upstairs the wind was pounding her house and through the narrow basement window she could see debris scooting across her lawn. A crash vibrated through the house and she shuddered, hunkering over the silent dog. A quick glance at the window and this time she saw only tree limbs against the glass.

The door slammed. Wind wailed outside, roaring like a train about to come off the tracks. More glass shattering. And then the windows in the basement. Lexi ducked as a pipe in the basement ceiling fell.

It was an old house, and the upstairs hardwood floor and underlying support beams were the ceiling for the basement. Pipes and electric wires crisscrossed the big, open room, making it not the safest place to be in a tornado. She preferred the storage room in the far corner of the basement.

"Lexi, here it is." Colt took the last step and was halfway across the room when the house above them splintered and crackled. "Run to the storage room."

Colt's voice was drowned out by the roaring wind. He reached them, grabbing the dog and pushing behind her. A board splintered and fell. Lexi tried to duck, but the board hit the arm she lifted to shield herself and then it hit her head.

Crashing and roaring filled her ears and the world tilted. Colt was behind her, pushing her forward.

"Don't fall, Lexi. Keep moving."

"I can't." She was dizzy and her eyes clouded for a second. Her legs buckled and she felt Colt's arm against hers. Her ears popped and her lungs heaved for air. "I can't."

"Five more steps. You can." He shoved with his shoulder and they were in the storage room, the door slamming behind him. The building shuddered around them.

A house over one hundred years old and today it gave up. Lexi cried because the house had history. The house had stood the test of time.

It was the one thing in her life that had been sturdy and unwavering. It had a history that she had wanted, of families growing up and growing old together. As she ran to the far corner of the room, she knew the house was falling in around them.

Her ears were filled with the sound of glass shattering and wood splintering, and behind her, the ragged breath of her ex-husband as he moved them to safety.

"You're bleeding." Colt laid the dog on the floor and glanced over his shoulder as Lexi dropped to the ground, leaning her head on her knees until her vision cleared. "Lexi, stay awake."

"Don't yell. My life is crumbling in around me and you're yelling."

"This is a house, not your life."

She watched as he slid the needle into the dog, the way she'd taught him. She missed their marriage. She missed him in the morning, waking her up with coffee, his hair tousled and more blond in the summer than the winter.

She missed getting up later than him. He'd be gone, but the bathroom would still smell like his deodorant and his cologne. She missed his scent on her pillow.

Her head really hurt. She bent, resting her forehead on knees she pulled to her chest.

"Stop." His voice was gruff, emotional.

"Stop what?" She looked up and blinked a few times. Pain throbbed and she touched her head. Her hand came away damp. She looked down at the blood on her fingers, mesmerized and confused.

"You're talking about the past, about us, like this is the end. This isn't the end, Lexi. We're both alive." Colt moved to her side, a folded towel in his hand. He dabbed at her head and then held the towel with pressure that made her wince.

"Not so hard." She bit down on her lip and looked up, meeting blue eyes that connected with hers and didn't look away. "I didn't know I was talking."

His laughter was soft and his eyes crinkled at

the corners. He kept the towel on her head. "You were talking, and I'm honored. But you need to stay awake."

"I'm awake." She leaned back against the wall and thought she felt it heave with the pressure of the storm and the falling building. "You should be out there, helping other people."

"I doubt I can do that right now. Let's talk. I know you can talk, even when you're tired."

"And you always fall asleep when I'm talking."

"Midnight isn't the best time for heartfelt conversations."

"When is the best time? Or is there ever a right time?" She leaned against his shoulder, her eyes focusing on the sleeping dog. "I love that dog."

"I'm sorry. Lexi, let's not talk about the past or the dog."

"We don't have a future, so what else do we talk about?" She felt a little sick to her stomach. He probably didn't want to hear that. "I'm going to be sick."

"Okay. It's okay." But he held her close, as if he was afraid she'd slip away. "Don't go to sleep, Lex."

"I'm not. It's just a…"

"A cut." He supplied the word. "Do you remember what day it is?"

"Tuesday?"

"Nope." He moved and slid away from her. "It's

Friday, July tenth. I'm going to see if I can call for help, or get us out of here."

"Don't leave me."

He paused, his hand on the door, his uniform covered in her blood and Chico's. "I'm not leaving you, Lex."

She would have nodded, but her head hurt when she moved. And hadn't he already left her? Hadn't he packed his bags and walked away? He shook his head, as if he knew her thoughts, and walked through the door. A few minutes later he was back. His clothes were now covered with white dust and dirt.

"Well?"

"We're trapped, I don't have cell service, and my radio isn't working." He slid down the wall and hooked his arm around her to pull her close. "The stairs are blocked with debris, and part of the basement has caved in."

"You'll save us. You always do."

"I wish that was true." He kissed her cheek. "I'm not sure how to get us out of this one."

"You're supposed to be positive." She leaned forward, sick, and her head ached. "I'm scared."

"Don't be. We'll be fine. We'll get out of here."

She closed her eyes and listened to a world that had become silent. The building groaned above them, creaking a little as the wreckage of her home settled. Warm tears slid down her cheeks. In the distance she heard sirens.

"Can you imagine if this is it for us? What if today was the last day we had?" She opened her eyes and looked up at him, wondering why she had let him go so easily.

"Listen, my optimistic sweetheart, that isn't you talking."

"It is me. I'm saying, what if this is how we told the story of our lives? That we gave up." She leaned against him, her head aching and nausea twisting her stomach. The words were definitely more maudlin than she'd intended.

"At least we're together." He murmured into her hair and his breath was soft and minty.

"Yes, together?" Her eyes were getting heavy and she didn't know if she could keep her promise to stay awake. "I'm so tired."

"Lexi, don't sleep." He sat her up, shaking her a little.

"Don't be so rough. I'm awake."

"Lexi, you have to stay with me. You can't go to sleep."

"What if we don't get out of here?" she whispered. "What if they don't find us in time?"

"They'll find us and we'll get out and go on with our lives." He held her close. "Hear that, sirens. Bud has called in the cavalry. They'll find us."

She shook her head and it ached, but Colt's arms were around her. She wanted to think of nothing but sinking into the darkness, with his arms around her, and the knowledge that God wouldn't let it end this way.

Her eyes closed and Colt gave her a gentle shake. When she whispered that she couldn't stay awake, he told her she had to. And then he pulled her close, and his lips touched hers, gentle and persuading. He held her close, making her feel safe. Tomorrow she would deal with losing him again, but for tonight, it was enough to be in his arms.

# Chapter One

Labor Day Weekend

The citizens of High Plains were getting back to normal. Or so they tried to say when they met for cleanup days and to plan community events. Days like today, when they planned to do more work on the town hall. The new Old Town Hall. It had been a building rich in history and a central part of the community. The tornado had leveled it.

Getting back to normal. The aftermath of the storm had left them anything but "normal." Lexi knew it, so did everyone else.

With the media long gone, along with volunteers who had—understandably—gone back to their own lives, the people in High Plains and the surrounding area were still trying to put the pieces of their lives back together.

High Plains, Kansas, was nothing more than a two-minute clip on the weather station's reel about deadly storms. But that clip didn't mention Jesse Logan's premature triplets, or the wife he'd lost. It didn't talk about Kasey, the child Gregory Garrison had found at the Waters cottages. The weather station didn't say anything about the people who had come to help, bringing food, supplies and prayers.

Those had been big stories for the first few weeks, and then they had faded out. Life had gone on. Other news, more current, had taken the place of those stories.

The weather station still showed the path of the storm, outtakes from local news and aerial shots from helicopters. Lexi hated to admit she'd watched it over and over again, still amazed by what had happened to her town while she'd been in her basement, safe in the arms of her ex-husband.

"Isn't that sweet," had become the catch phrase associated with the six hours she and Colt had been trapped down there.

People had asked if she and Colt had worked things out. There had been comments about God putting the two of them in that basement together. The only real outcome was that the two of them had made a decision to be friends. If they were going to live in the same town, friendship after two years of silence seemed like an improvement.

Lexi leaned against one of the few trees left standing in the yard of the Old Town Hall. The rest had been toppled in the tornado, along with half the town of High Plains. It was said that there wasn't a building in town that wasn't damaged in some way.

The lives of some of the citizens were not much better than the buildings. Including her own life.

They were all rebuilding.

Lexi closed her eyes, pushing aside those thoughts, instead enjoying the warmth of the afternoon sun on her face and the distant sound of children playing. She hadn't slept a lot last night. She rarely slept soundly, not in the metal building that housed her clinic. It was her house for now. She'd turned an unused corner into an apartment of sorts.

When she opened her eyes, her attention fell on those children that she'd heard. One of them was little Kasey. No one knew the identity of that poor little girl. They didn't know her name, where she came from or even her birthday.

The town called her Kasey, because the initials K.C. had been found inside her clothes.

Lexi wiped away the tears that still fell too easily. Every time she said she wouldn't cry anymore, something happened and the tears seemed to have a mind of their own.

A blue Jeep Cherokee cruised down Main Street

and stopped in front of the construction site. Lexi watched Colt get out of the vehicle, his uniform starched and perfect as if he controlled even the wrinkles and made them bend to his will. He slipped on leather gloves and walked toward her. And her heart reacted. She didn't want it to, but it did.

Six hours in her basement with him and she'd realized something—she hadn't moved on. She realized that signing her name on a line didn't undo her love for him. But realizing that the feelings still existed didn't undo her fear that he might walk out on her again.

Her life had crumbled around her on that day in July. She could focus only on rebuilding one thing at a time. For now, she needed to rebuild her house and help rebuild her town.

Or move back to Manhattan, Kansas. That was her parents' recommendation for starting over. And sometimes she thought it sounded like a good idea.

"What are you doing here?" Colt asked as he approached. Out of nowhere, Chico appeared. The dog must have been running loose again.

She slipped her hand over the dog's head and down his neck. His side had healed with nothing but a scar to show for his injury. He still whimpered from time to time, but he was fine.

"Well?" He prodded, moving her from the past to the present.

"I'm assigned to town hall duty today. I'm stacking stones from the old foundation so they can be used in the new steps and the sidewalk."

"Imagine that, so am I."

"If they're trying to push us together, it's your fault for getting stuck in the basement with me."

"I'm willing to let them talk." He winked, proving his point. "Well, we'd better get busy if we're going to have this building finished for Christmas."

She nodded, because she didn't know what to say. They had been assigned to the same job. She glanced in the direction of Reverend Michael Garrison, who had obviously planned this little encounter between herself and Colt. The minister had the good sense to turn a little red and walk away. People who had figured out the path to true love were always trying to help others find their way.

A smile sneaked up on her, because she couldn't stay mad at Michael. Instead she pulled her gloves back on and walked away from Colt. He followed, as she had known he would.

"Time to get busy." She grabbed a stone and stacked it on the pile for single stones, unbroken. Others were too far gone to use. Those pieces were being piled up to be hauled away, along with broken glass and wood that had been dozed into a pile that was awaiting a dump truck to haul it off.

"What about the wood flooring that is still intact?" Colt picked up a strip of stained wood that had once been the floor inside the town hall.

"We're keeping those, too. They're going to find a use for them inside the new building. I think the wood is being stored at Garrison's, in the lumberyard."

Colt set the board aside, his gaze sweeping the area. "We're moving forward. They're starting the framing of the building next week."

"Yes, I know." She didn't look at him.

"How is your house?" He tossed a few pieces of crumbled limestone into the pile of debris that was growing larger and larger every day.

"They dozed it down yesterday. I found a contractor. He hauled in a trailer and he's working in the area. He's taken on several projects, so who knows how long this will take." She ignored the look he shot her. He thought she didn't know what she was doing.

"Did you check him out?"

"Yes, Colt, I checked him out. He had references."

"I'm sorry, but you know how it is when something like this happens. Scam artists come out of the woodwork." He nodded and pushed at some rocks with his booted foot. "Watch for snakes."

"I know." She glanced up, wishing that September had brought cooler weather. She took off her gloves and swiped her hair from her face.

"Are you mad?" he asked, with a characteristic male it-can't-be-me attitude.

"No, not at all. But trust me that I can take care of this, of having the house rebuilt." She turned, smiling and wishing immediately that she hadn't looked at him. He was the son of a rancher and he looked as good in a uniform with a sidearm attached to his waist as he did in jeans and T-shirts, loading bags of grain into the back of a truck.

The uniform was unusual. It must have been a court day because on regular days he wore dark jeans and a dark T-shirt with Police in white letters across the back. She really liked that uniform.

"You are mad."

His words were an unfair reminder that she shouldn't be thinking of him in his uniform. She shouldn't be thinking of him at all, except to be angry with him.

"I'm not mad." She was confused and hurt. She'd spent six hours in a basement, wondering if they would get out and if they had let go of something they should have fought harder to keep. He didn't want to hear that.

True to form, Colt grabbed the wheelbarrow

and headed for the pile of rocks she had started earlier in the day. That was his way of saying they weren't going to talk about it—discussion closed.

He dumped the load of stones, and then turned. "Lexi, I can't do this."

"Can't do this?" She glanced around, at the stones, at the mess, knowing that wasn't what he meant.

"We can't go back. We have to move forward."

She nodded, wondering if that meant he had felt something in that basement, too. Had those hours made him question their divorce? But he wouldn't talk. She knew that, because this was as far as their conversations ever went. They wouldn't talk about the divorce or their feelings for one another. They had never talked about Gavin's death and what that had meant to their marriage or the family they had planned to have.

She couldn't blame it all on him. Her own fears, the thought of losing Colt the way Gavin's wife had lost him, had added to the problem.

She followed his gaze to the open green area between Main Street and the High Plains River. There were still piles of debris to be cleaned up. The path of the storm had been long and wide.

Lexi's most recent phone bill had been found thirty miles away. Someone had called to let her know that it was being sent back. Others had found their family photos, tax documents and receipts scattered in fields and nearby towns.

All over town, people were starting over. They were rebuilding. Or they were moving on.

Lexi was sharing her home with animals that had been found wandering the area. Many hadn't been claimed.

"We need to get to work." Colt picked up a stone. "Don't forget your gloves."

She started to remind him that she wasn't his to take care of. Instead she pulled on the gloves she had shoved into her pockets. What she wanted to do was remind him of their discussion in the basement. Even with a head injury, she hadn't forgotten that they were going to stop fighting. They were going to be friends.

Colt moved closer, his gaze drifting past her and then back to her face. "Lex, there's too much going on around here. We have a child without parents. Jesse Logan's wife is dead and his babies had to fight to survive. We have a town that needs our help rebuilding."

"I know. But, Colt, we can work together without it being weird. We really can be friends."

He nodded and looked away again. "How are you feeling?"

"I'm fine." She touched the scar at her hairline. "The headaches are gone."

"Good, I'm glad. I'm glad your mom came to help you after you got out of the hospital."

"She stayed a few days."

"At least she came."

Yes, Lexi's mom had visited. And she'd spent three days telling Lexi what a huge mistake every detail of her life had been. Marrying Colt, a mistake. Becoming a veterinarian, bigger mistake. Staying in High Plains after her divorce, the biggest mistake.

Lexi smiled again. "Snake."

Colt jumped and turned. No snake. He shot her a look and then he smiled. "Cute, real cute."

"I still think it's funny that you can square off with bad guys, brave a tornado, and yet you're afraid of a little ole snake."

"They bite."

"Right." She reached for a block. It crumbled in her hands and she tossed it into the pile of debris.

"Did you know that the town hall was destroyed by a tornado in 1860?" Colt pushed the wheelbarrow a few feet.

"I did know that. High Plains had to rebuild after that storm, and we'll rebuild again. We're tough people. We're pioneers. It's in our blood." She wiped her brow. "And we have a lot of faith."

"Yes, faith." His voice turned sarcastic. "And God rewarded us with this." A wide sweep of his arm took in the destruction that had once been a town.

"God didn't do this, Colt. You know that." She didn't want to have the faith argument with him, not now. Hers was still too new, still growing.

"I know He didn't. I just question why He allowed so many people to suffer, to be hurt."

"No one has an answer to why bad things happen. But look at the people who were protected. He put Tommy in front of Gregory Garrison's office at the right moment, in time to be saved. What if he had been somewhere else? What if I had gone to my basement? What if Chico hadn't been running loose, and you hadn't brought him to me? Where would you have been?"

"We still can't find Tommy's dog." Colt said it like a last-ditch attempt at proving her faith wrong.

"I'm praying Tommy's dog is out there. We've found other animals that we thought were lost for good."

"That's the difference between me and you, Lexi. You have faith that He really is up there, taking time for us. I look at this town and wonder where He was that day in July when we needed Him. I wonder where He was when Gavin got shot on that highway outside of town."

"He was there with Gavin, and now Gavin is with Him." She flinched against the anger in Colt's eyes, but she didn't back down. "And on that day in July, He was sheltering a little girl this town named Kasey, and watching over a boy named Tommy."

"So He saved some and not others. Look at this ravaged building, right next to the church, but the church is still standing."

"I think you lost that argument. The church *is* still standing. Solid. I think that sometimes bad things happen and we find faith to get through, to find purpose and to move on."

"Is that what you've done, found faith?"

"Yes, I've found faith, Colt. I've found what I spent my childhood searching for." And what she thought she'd find in a marriage to him. It had taken divorce for faith to become real in her life. "And whether you want to admit it or not, you still have faith. You've just buried it beneath anger and resentment."

"I can't have this conversation right now."

"I know, and I'm sorry. I didn't mean to preach."

He laughed and leaned, his forehead resting against hers. "Yes, you did."

No, she hadn't. But it felt good, to be able to defend what she believed. Church was more than a place she went to hide. It was more than the fairy tale she'd believed in as a child, the place she went to, looking for a happy-ever-after.

Finding faith was the one good thing that came out of her divorce.

\* \* \*

Colt knew that he should back away from Lexi. But he couldn't. He had almost lost her in that tornado. Not a day went by that he didn't think about that, and about his life without her in it. But she wasn't really in his life, not now. He had made that choice, to separate and then divorce.

He stepped back, aware as always that she was beautiful. She was a city girl who wore blazers and scarves. She had come to him with everything, and nothing. She had wanted a family. And babies.

She wanted lots of babies.

His guilt, over not getting to Gavin on time, had been a wedge that drove them apart. He had faced God with anger. She had retreated into faith, believing everything would be okay.

He hadn't wanted to fail her, not Lexi with her silky brown hair that hung in a curtain past her shoulders. She parted it on the side and it had a way of falling forward when she worked. It was the sweetest and the sexiest thing he'd ever seen. He sighed and moved away from her.

"Colt, don't walk away."

He walked back to her side, took her hand and led her away from the building site where curious eyes watched and a few people whispered and nodded in their direction.

He knew what those people were saying. The

whole town was talking about the two of them getting back together. As if it meant something to find them buried in that basement together.

"Remember what you said on our first date?" He let go of her hand.

"I wanted a real family, the kind that went to church together and took walks. I was a kid, Colt. I had dreams of what a perfect family looked like. I didn't know then what I know now, that there's more to it."

"And I promised to give you that family." He hadn't.

A few years ago, they had been talking about having children. Colt had embraced the idea, picturing a little girl with her eyes and his hair. Or maybe the other way around. Definitely a girl with Lexi's heart.

He saw movement out of the corner of his eye and turned as Reverend Garrison walked up. Reverend. It was still hard to call Michael by that title.

"Hey, how are the two of you doing over here?" Michael picked up a stone and stacked it on the pile. "Some of these stones are engraved with dates of the first settlers' weddings. If you see them, try to separate them. I think they would be perfect for the landscaping project."

Colt didn't answer. He gave his friend a look and went back to stacking blocks. Michael had found a way to remind Colt that he and Lexi had been married here.

"We're just reminiscing, Michael." Lexi smoothed her hair back from her face and gave Colt a look that he'd seen before.

"There's a lot of that going on." Michael Garrison stopped working and pulled off his gloves. Colt ignored his matchmaking friend. Michael had brought up—more than once—that Colt and Lexi had spent six long hours stuck in that basement, the two of them and God. Maybe that had been God's way of giving them time alone to work on their relationship.

Michael never left God out of the equation. That made Colt a little itchy around his neck.

"We've got a lot to get done." Colt stacked more blocks in the wheelbarrow.

"Snake." Michael pointed. Colt wasn't fooled. He'd already fallen for Lexi's little joke.

And then it hissed. Colt jumped back, and Michael laughed. Lexi's laughter was soft, a little husky. He glanced her way and tried to pretend the snake didn't matter. It slithered away and he reached for another block.

"We're having a Labor Day picnic here on Sunday after church." Michael said it as if it meant something. "We could use some help with the grills."

Of course. Colt had known it had to be something. "I can help. What time do you want me to be here?"

"Church starts at eleven."

Colt glanced from his ex-wife to what could soon be his ex-friend. Colt hadn't been to church since before the divorce. Since Gavin's death.

His partner's death wasn't the only thing that had driven the wedge between him and God. Somewhere along the way, he'd gotten angry. He just hadn't gotten it, the whole God thing.

He couldn't forget an auction from when he was a kid, when land from his family farm had been sold off, piece by piece.

Church at eleven. Lexi watched him, teeth holding her bottom lip and blue eyes wide, waiting. He wasn't going to make a promise that he might not keep. All of his life he had been proud that his word was good, it was solid. People could count on him to be there for them.

Sometimes he let them down.

"Colt, you don't have to come to church." Michael stacked another stone and moved away. "But you can be here to cook. You're not getting out of that."

"I'll be here."

Lexi was still looking at him, as if she wanted more from him. His radio crackled, and Bud's voice filtered into his ear.

"I have to go. There's a dog wandering in a field outside of town. It might be Tommy's."

"Let me know if you need me. If it's a stray, I have room in the kennel."

"The ark, you mean. That place of yours is starting to get attention from the city council."

"The animals have to be taken care of. Maybe you should try the animal shelter idea on them again. This might help them to see how much we need a place for strays and unwanted pets."

He brushed hair back from her face and found it easy to smile. "Don't ever change, Lex."

"I haven't changed, Colt." Lexi's whispered words caught up with him as he walked away and he nodded, because he didn't know what to say. And she was wrong. She had changed.

She was stronger than ever, proving she didn't really need him.

## Chapter Two

Colt drove out of town, in the general direction of the area where the dog had been spotted. As he drove, he could see the faded—and sometimes ripped—signs that Tommy had put up right after the tornado, when they first realized Charlie was missing.

Gregory Garrison had searched the area, looking for that dog. He'd even tried a new puppy. Nothing worked. Tommy only wanted the original Charlie. Colt didn't blame the kid. That dog had been the boy's family.

As he drove, he passed where Marie Logan's body had been found. Colt had insisted on being the one to give Jesse the news about his wife. He remembered the look on Jesse's face. The disbelief. Maybe a little betrayal. What a thing for a man to go through, finding a Dear John letter and then something like that happening.

Colt pulled up to the farmhouse that had once been beautiful and well maintained. Time and age had started the deterioration of the place. The storm had done the rest. The chicken houses that had helped provide when times were lean had been ripped off their foundations in the tornado and strips of sheet metal were blown across the county. Some of those pieces of metal were still wrapped around trees.

The old farmer came out of the house, bib overalls and work boots. Colt stepped out of his car and met the other man in the middle of the yard.

"Hey, Walter, how are you?"

Walter, worn and haggard, shrugged slim shoulders. "Seen better days, Colt. Seen better days. Drought last year and now this. It makes it hard to be a farmer."

"Yeah, it does." Colt looked around, at barns and outbuildings that looked as run-down as the farmer standing in front of him.

"I thought they'd send a county officer, not the town chief of police."

"The city voted to extend the city limits out a mile, Walter. I can usually get here sooner than county, anyway. So, about that dog."

"I seen a dog, back in the field. It was a shaggy

brown thing. I heard in church that they're still looking for that boy's dog. I couldn't remember what it looked like."

"I'll drive out through your field and take a look. But it doesn't sound like Charlie. Walter, are you doing okay out here?"

His wife had passed away a year ago. His kids had moved off, finding jobs in town and giving up life on the farm. Colt remembered when he had wanted to trade farming for anything but farming.

"I'm doing all right." But his gaunt appearance worried Colt.

"Are you going to keep the farm? Some of the people who took hits as hard as yours are talking about selling out."

"Nah, I ain't going anywhere. This is all I know. At least I have a roof over my head. It's a little leaky now, but it's a roof."

"Leaky?"

"Well, seems it was damaged by the tornado."

"Have you contacted your insurance?"

The old farmer sighed. "I did, but I guess there's a problem with my policy."

"Walter, did you tell anyone?" Colt's face got a little hot.

"I tried to call some government office, but got put on hold. And you know I can't hear on the phone."

"Let's take a look around this place." Colt

started walking and Walter followed, slower than he used to be, stepping a little more cautiously. How many older farmers like Walter were being ripped off or ignored?

As they walked, Colt realized that a window in the back bedroom of the old farmhouse was still busted and the little leak in the roof was big enough for a basketball to fit through. Shingles were gone from another section.

Someone had to get out here and do something. Colt should have done something. He just hadn't realized. There were so many people needing assistance it was hard to keep up with who had been taken care of, and who hadn't.

"Walter, I'm going to make some calls for you, but in the meantime, I've still got some tarps in my Jeep that I keep on hand for situations like this. Let's get a tarp over your roof and a piece of plywood over that window."

"I sure appreciate that, Colt, but you don't have to. I called my boy, and he's coming down in a week or two. He told me to call you, but I told him it could wait."

"Walter, you should have called."

The older farmer looked down at boots that were scuffed and worn. Those boots of his probably took on water just like the roof.

Colt pulled his cell phone out of his pocket. "I

have to make a call, but how about a sandwich? I have a couple in my lunch box."

"I can't take your lunch."

"Nonsense. I stick it in there in case I get stuck on a call, but I didn't need it today." Colt opened the car door and pulled out the lunch box and grabbed a bottle of water out of the cooler in the back of his rig. "Go have a seat on the front porch and I'll be right with you."

He watched Walter hobble away and then he pulled out his cell phone and dialed Michael Garrison.

"Michael, this is Colt. I'm out at Walter's farm…."

"Is it Charlie?"

"I haven't seen the dog yet. But Walter really needs some assistance out here. I'm going to put a tarp on his roof and board up a window that got blown out, but he's having problems with insurance. I'm not sure if he even has food."

"I'll get right on it, Colt. You're a good man. And thanks for volunteering to cook on Sunday."

"Volunteering my…"

"Foot," Michael provided.

"Yes, my foot." Colt ended the conversation. Sunday, church and Lexi. He'd rather walk on glass than face her and God on the same day, in the same place.

* * *

Sunday morning Lexi stood on the steps of the church, waiting, and still praying Colt would show up. People passed her on the steps, some smiling or saying hello, others involved in their own thoughts, or conversations with the person next to them. They didn't notice her alone on the steps.

Standing there on the steps, she realized that more than the landscape had changed since the tornado. People had changed. Lives had really changed. She watched as Nicki Appleton, a preschool teacher in town, got out of her car with Kasey, the toddler that Gregory Garrison had found at the Waters cottages near the river.

The child held tight to Nicki's hand, and looked for all the world as if they belonged together. What would happen to Nicki's heart when the little girl's family was found? Lexi didn't want to think about that, or the pain the child's leaving would cause.

Instead she focused on Heather Waters, standing next to Pastor Michael—as Lexi liked to think of the reverend. He just seemed more down-to-earth and reachable than the title Reverend implied. The two, Heather and Michael, had found love, lost love, after the tornado. They gave her hope for her own life, her own broken relationship.

And Maya Logan and Gregory Garrison. The

two had fallen in love and were getting married. Two very different people, and the tornado had brought them together and made the differences melt away. They were going to adopt little Tommy and give him a forever family.

Footsteps behind her. Lexi turned in time to see Michael's niece, Avery, slinking past her. The teenager looked as if she was up to something. The girl had been doing so much better since she came to High Plains to stay with Michael; the return of this sneaky side surprised Lexi.

"How is school going, Avery?" Lexi stopped the girl.

Avery's mouth opened and she blinked, but then she smiled. She was a pretty girl, fresh-faced and not at all the dark teen she had tried to be at one time.

"Oh, good. You know, just hanging out."

"I could still use help feeding dogs, if you'd like."

"Umm, yeah, maybe sometime. Heather's keeping me pretty busy."

"Good. Well, maybe when you have more time."

Avery nodded and darted off.

Lexi's friend Jill walked out the door and stood next to her. They had prayed together the previous evening, not just for Colt, but for the community and the hearts and lives that were still healing.

"He'll be here." Jill squeezed Lexi's hand. "He can run from God, but he can't hide."

"He didn't say he would come to church."

"But he might." Jill, always optimistic.

Lexi smiled, but it wasn't easy. Her life was hanging in the balance, waiting for the pieces to come together again. For a long time she had waited, thinking Colt would come back to her. As much as it hurt, she was starting to accept that maybe his coming home wasn't the best thing for her. Last night, for the first time, she had prayed about moving on without him.

She still wanted him to have faith. Even if he wasn't in her life.

Jill hugged her. "I have to get inside. Will you be okay?"

"I'm okay. I'll be inside in just a second."

"Okay. Gotta run, though. The choir is getting settled and I can see Linda looking for me. She's not smiling."

"She never smiles." Lexi turned to look inside the church at Linda, who really was a happy and loving person. The choir was her place in church. She'd been there for nearly fifty years. "Go, I'll be fine."

"I know you will." One last squeeze of her hand and then Jill walked away.

Lexi stood in the doorway for a few minutes, waiting until the last second before she turned and walked inside. Colt hadn't shown up. She shrugged off disappointment. Like so many other times in her life, she told herself that it didn't matter.

People weren't always there when you expected or needed them. She had learned that early on from parents who had been busy with careers; their child had been an afterthought. It had almost become that way with Colt and his job. He had been obsessed with catching the guy that shot Gavin.

Lexi sat down in her customary pew and opened the hymnal. Her vision blurred a little and she blinked to clear the mist. It was lonely, walking in by herself, watching families take their seats, settling children on their laps or next to them with crayons and pieces of paper or coloring books.

She had always wanted to be one of those families. As a kid she had gone to church with neighbors, the Clines, because her parents had been busy with their real estate business and hadn't had time. Sundays her parents did brunch and talked to prospective clients.

The Cline family had been her ideal family. They had played basketball in the evenings, and they walked their dogs together. They had gone to church together every Sunday and every Wednesday. And when she had eaten dinner with them, they had joined hands and prayed.

She had wanted that family. For a lot of years

that family, more than faith, had been what she longed for.

She sighed and closed her eyes. Footsteps caught her attention and then a movement and someone scooting in next to her. She looked up, swallowing delight and fear as Colt sat next to her.

"Stop looking at me like that, Lexi." He reached for a hymnal and glanced at the one she held before flipping to the correct page.

For the first time in a long time, she had someone next to her. But she still felt alone. She was alone. Colt had a house on the other side of town and she had a divorce decree in her safe.

Colt sat through the sermon, his ex-wife next to him, and a couple of hundred pairs of eyes glancing occasionally in their direction. Due to the renewed attendance of the faithful, extra chairs had been hauled into the sanctuary to create more seating. Even Dan Garrison, Greg's dad, was in attendance. Colt figured Dan had been out of church longer than he had.

The disaster of the tornado had brought out church members that hadn't darkened the doors in years.

He knew because when he patrolled on Sundays he saw the overflowing parking lot. He had seen it before; a disaster brought new congregants, and the return of old. Some stayed in church. After a few months, most of them would go back to Sunday sports and forget promises to God.

Promises—to God, to Lexi and to himself. Those were the promises that Colt remembered. The day of the tornado, when Lexi lost consciousness for a short period of time, he had made some bargains with God.

He had made promises that he didn't know how to keep.

He pulled at the back of his collar and moved in the seat as his attention wavered and then was pulled back to Michael Garrison's sermon. The words were the same as so many other sermons, about trusting God in good times and bad. But there was some honesty that took Colt by surprise. Everyone has doubts from time to time. God can handle it. God can't always undo the reality of life on this planet, but He can give us faith to get through. What we have to do is rely on Him, even when doubts arise.

Colt had plenty of doubts. He closed his eyes, remembering how it felt to drive up on Gavin's patrol car that night, and to find his friend, a county officer, on the highway, bleeding—gasping for his last breath.

Powerless to help, Colt had cried out to God. He remembered that moment, kneeling on the highway, promising his friend things—promising to pray, promising to take care of a man's wife.

He had made bargains that night, too. As if he could make deals with God.

A hand rested on his arm. He lifted his head and opened his eyes. Lexi sat next to him, real, breathing and no longer a part of his life. Not really.

"You okay?"

"What?" He looked around. The sermon was over, people were standing up.

"I asked if you're okay. I know this isn't easy."

"But I'm here."

"You're here." She looked far too hopeful.

"I'm here because I promised. And because I have to cook."

"Poor Colt, always being held hostage by that sense of commitment you prize."

"Sarcasm isn't you, Lexi." He stood and she followed him toward the back door. He had parked his car back there and he had seen the grills already set up and ready to go.

"Maybe it's the new me." Relentless, Lexi kept up with him.

"I don't think so." He turned, smiling because she looked pretty in the deep blue dress and high heels. She was thin and tanned, and her hair hung like silk past her shoulders.

"Any leads on the identity of the little girl,

Kasey?" She asked the question out of the blue. But not. Of course she'd want to know about a child.

He opened the door for her, and she slid through. He followed, out into bright afternoon sunshine and dry, late-summer heat. The charcoal in the grills had been lit and a few men were already cooking burgers.

Colt opened a cooler and pulled out a box of premade hamburger patties. Lexi stood at his side, waiting for an answer.

"No, I haven't learned anything. I put articles in papers from surrounding areas, and the national news covered it a few weeks ago."

"I saw that. You would think someone would be claiming the precious little thing."

"Her parents are out there somewhere. I just hope they're…" He couldn't say it. Lexi nodded; she understood. They all hoped and prayed that the child's parents were alive.

But if they were alive, what did that say about them? A living, breathing, caring parent would have claimed her. Right?

Or grandparents.

"You'll find her family." Lexi broke apart a few frozen burgers. He placed them on the grill as she handed them over.

"I don't know, Lexi. I feel like I haven't done enough."

"You always feel that way, Colt. You've done everything, and you're still beating yourself up, thinking the whole world needs you to take care of it." She shot him a dark blue look of accusation in eyes that shimmered and then didn't.

She was a lot stronger than he'd ever given her credit for.

When they first met, back in college, he'd treated her like a china doll that needed to be taken care of. Now she took care of thousand-pound horses and wrestled with sick cows. Today she looked like a princess. Tomorrow he'd probably see her in that truck of hers, wearing a stained T-shirt, faded jeans and work boots.

He smiled and he hadn't meant to.

Lexi smiled back. She backed a step away, a retreat, still smiling. She looked like someone who had just won a battle. He didn't know what he'd lost or what ground she'd gained. But somehow it mattered.

"I'm going to help with the children. They're blowing bubbles." Lexi touched his arm, her hand sliding down to his, pausing there for a minute and then breaking contact.

"Okay." He could have said more, but he would have stammered. Not the way for a man to prove he was in control of a situation.

He watched her walk away, pulling her hair

back with a clip as she went. He remembered those clips and how he used to like to pull them loose as she leaned over her desk.

At one time he would have leaned over her and kissed her neck, and she would have smiled, but pretended to ignore him.

"Colt, your grill's on fire."

Startled back to the moment he reached for the spray bottle of water and squirted the flaming coals. A quick glance over his shoulder and he saw Lexi turn to smile at him.

Lexi smiled as she watched Colt with the spray bottle, putting out the fire that had erupted in the grill. She liked seeing him not in control of a situation. He got a little scattered when it happened, because it happened so rarely. When he looked back at her, she nodded and turned away. Happy, because she had been the one to scramble his self-control.

She skipped away to the area where children of all ages were playing with all different types of bubble-blowing contraptions. In the open lawn area of the church others were flying kites and throwing Frisbees.

"Why the frown when you were smiling a few minutes ago?"

Jill. Lexi glanced at her friend who had left the

small group she'd been talking to and was now at Lexi's side.

"I didn't mean to frown." Lexi looked around the lawn at the people, and past to the buildings that were still damaged. "If you could focus on just this one spot, on the people having fun here, you could fool yourself into believing the tornado never happened."

"I know. Sometimes I look out my window and it's like I live somewhere else, somewhere other than the town I grew up in." Jill smiled at a little girl who ran up to them with an unopened bottle of bubbles. "Do you need for me to open it?"

The child nodded, and Jill opened the bubbles and handed them back. The little girl scooted off, and Lexi didn't know where else to go with the conversation, not when her mind kept turning back to the six hours in her basement with Colt holding her close.

Six hours that had given her hope that maybe, just maybe, she and Colt could work out their problems and rebuild their marriage.

As the workers dug them out that night, Colt had stayed by her side. He had held her close, whispering reassurances. He had stayed with her until they loaded her into the back of the ambulance. Alone, it had been hard to remain optimistic, believing his whispered promise.

She could still close her eyes and see his face in the window of the ambulance and hear the hand that had hit the door, giving them the okay to pull away. And when she woke up in the Manhattan hospital, it had been her mother's face, not Colt's.

Nothing had changed in that basement.

Let it go, she told herself. Today was a day of rebuilding, not reliving the past. Moving forward, that was the sermon's title. Moving forward, knowing God is still in control and still able to answer prayers.

She had to let it go, because she still wanted more than Colt could give her. She wanted to be somewhere on the top of his list of priorities, not the person that came after everyone else.

She didn't want to be the person waiting, wondering if he would come home.

It was hard to put that into words. In their marriage, she had failed to explain it to him. It had come out as accusations. She knew that, now. Too late.

"Come on, let's play horseshoes." Lexi's friend Jill nudged her from the memories.

Jill, in her prairie skirt and boots, was a cowgirl. The real deal, not the city kind, like Lexi. Jill could rope, shoot a gun and make cheese. Of course she would beat Lexi at a game like horseshoes.

"I'm not sure about horseshoes," Lexi admitted. "I'm better at blowing bubbles."

Jill reached for a bottle of bubbles on a table. "Go for it, then. But I see a certain cowboy that I've been after for about ten years. You blow bubbles and I'll see you later."

"Watch out for that cowboy," Lexi warned. "He'll break your heart."

Jill shrugged and danced away, her skirt swishing around her legs.

Lexi dipped the plastic wand into the bubbles and drew it out. Rather than blowing, she waved it in a circle. Huge bubbles flew through the air, floating and then landing on the grass, some popping midair.

Children ran around, hands out, trying to catch the illusive bubbles. Little girls with pigtails and boys with crew cuts.

"Lexi, I need to ask a favor." Michael Garrison walked toward her, weaving his way through the crowd of bubble-blowing children, who now saw him as a target. He laughed, swatting at bubbles and ruffling the hair of the children surrounding him.

"Okay, a favor." She felt a little sick to her stomach, because he had that smile on his face. He was up to something.

"We're trying to match pets with people. I know you're about full over at the clinic, and a few other folks in town are taking in strays, so I thought this might be a way to match up lost pets to owners, or adopt them out. We might even do a rabies clinic while we're at it, just to make sure the pets are immunized."

It sounded good, but that mysterious twinkle in his eyes was another matter altogether. Lexi looked from Reverend Garrison to Colt, and wondered if there was a connection between them and this pet-matching project.

"If you're too busy…" Michael Garrison caught a bubble and it popped.

"What day and I'll make sure that I'm not."

"Next Saturday."

"Here at the church?" She looked around, and it didn't take long to realize that this was about the only place in town for a project like this one.

"Yes, at the church. We're trying hard to make this a comfortable place for people, so they feel good about coming and bringing their families. We all need to heal."

"Yes, we do."

"Oh, and don't forget the lost-and-found room. It's been filled up and emptied two or three times since it started. I know you lost so much…."

Lexi nodded, and she didn't cry this time when she thought about the house she and Colt had picked and furnished together. Most of her belongings had been destroyed, everything but a few pictures and a box of jewelry that had been her grandmother's. Even her wedding pictures had disappeared.

And her wedding ring set. She tried not to think about the engagement ring that Colt had put on her finger so many years ago, or the wedding ring they had picked out together. They'd been in a box in the hall closet.

Michael was still standing next to her.

"No sign of the Logan ring?" Lexi placed her bottle of bubbles into the hands of a little blonde with large blue eyes and dimples.

"Nothing. Some jewelry has shown up, but not the ring. Or Tommy's dog."

Tommy. Her gaze lingered on the boy, whose hand was held by the strong and powerful hand of Gregory Garrison. Now that was a wonderful tribute to God's care for the little ones.

"I know. I've had my eyes out for that dog." Lexi turned her attention back to the reverend. "Is it wrong to pray that a dog comes home?"

Michael shook his head. "I don't think so. Remember 'All Creatures Great and Small.'"

"'The Lord God made them all.'"

"And not only does He care about that dog, He cares about broken hearts."

Lexi looked up, shocked by the words. Her surprise must have registered. Michael smiled. "Tommy's heart, Lexi. That dog was his family when he didn't have one. I know he has one now, but the dog is still important to him."

"Yes, of course."

Michael shifted, looking away for a moment before looking back at her, a reverend again, not a young man, uncomfortable with the conversation.

"Don't give up." He said it with conviction and she was lost, because there were several things she could tag with that saying.

"Give up?"

"On Colt."

She blew out a sigh and looked away. "We gave up two years ago, Michael."

But she could admit to herself that in the crumbled remains of her house—that night in the basement—she had wondered if they could work things out. She had wanted him to stay with her that night.

And he had repeated history by sending her off in the ambulance alone. Alone.

She didn't want that to be the epitaph of her life: She Loved a Man, But Was Always Alone. Yuck, how depressing. But looking around High Plains with crumbled buildings and shattered lives, she put her marriage in that category. Some things couldn't be rebuilt. Like her marriage, they were beyond fixing.

"Where there's faith, Lexi, there's hope."

Michael still stood next to her, and his smile was soft but firm.

"Of course." She remembered Michael's sermon of two weeks ago. God doesn't make mistakes. He isn't taken by surprise, either.

Her marriage hadn't been a mistake. She still believed that God had brought her and Colt together. The divorce was another matter altogether. But it hadn't been her choice. She'd let Colt go, because she knew that she couldn't force him to stay.

He left her long before he actually walked out.

## Chapter Three

Colt rounded the corner of the church and found Lexi sitting on the back of her truck eating a burger drenched in ketchup and looking off in the direction of the river. It wasn't much of a river, not now with the floodwaters receding and normal, dry September weather depriving it of rain.

She looked up, and he smiled, lifting his plate. "I thought maybe I could find a seat next to you."

"I think we might be able to find you a place to sit." She pointed to the tailgate of the truck.

"Feels a lot like our first date." He sat down, leaning a little against the side of the truck so he could look at her.

"You took me to a soccer game in a field next to the apartment you lived in."

"You have to admit, you never forgot."

"No, I never forgot. You missed the goal and sprained your knee."

He hadn't forgotten, either. He still remembered the way she had sat next to him, perched on the tailgate of his truck, her dark hair blowing in the wind and the scent of strawberries and springtime circling and teasing his senses. He had fallen in love with her that day.

He hadn't planned for this moment to be a replica of the afternoon that had first brought them together. This had been an easy, uninvolved way to spend time with her. He hadn't meant for it to snare his heart.

"What's this all about, Colt. We've hardly talked since the tornado."

"Friendship, remember. I didn't forget, Lexi. I know what we talked about in the basement. We live in the same town, and we have to be around each other." He stared at the place where the gazebo had once stood, and he remembered kissing her there. "Sometimes I miss you."

He missed her all the time. Every day. He had thought that after two years, missing her would be easier. It wasn't.

"Sometimes I miss you, too. But I've missed you for three years."

Since Gavin's death, a year before their divorce. He couldn't let this moment become something more than he meant it to be. He didn't want to mislead her. He didn't want to let her down, either.

"Lex, I can't make promises that…"

"We'll work things out?"

He sighed, because she could still finish his sentences. How could he put walls between them and help her to move on when she constantly filled his thoughts and took up space in his heart?

"I want so much for you to have everything." He didn't know what else to say, and he knew she deserved a better explanation. But explaining his fears, admitting to the choking anxiety, that wasn't easy to do.

The cell phone attached to his belt jangled. He set his plate down to answer it. Lexi watched, waiting for him to hang up.

"That was Michael." He dropped the phone into his shirt pocket. "He went in to check the lost and found, and he found what looks like the Logan ring."

"The ring? Why would someone put it in the box?" She tossed her last bite of hamburger a distance away and picked up her soda can. "If someone had the Logan ring, they'd just give it back. Everyone in town knows who it belongs to."

Colt laughed. "All good questions, Lexi. And as the chief of police for High Plains, I plan on finding the answer to each and every one of them."

He tossed his plate in the nearby trash barrel.

When he turned, Lexi was behind him. She smiled. "I'm going with you."

He shook his head. "I think I can handle this one on my own."

"Men never pay attention to details."

"Details are my life, Lex."

The set tilt of her chin warned him he wasn't going to give her the brush-off. "I'm not letting you off the hook."

"This isn't a game."

Neatly plucked eyebrows arched. "No, but you're not going to get away from me this easily, Colt Ridgeway. I'm coming with you."

"Fine, let's go."

He led her through the back door of the church and down the hallway to Michael's office. The door was open a crack, and Colt could see Michael inside, sitting behind his desk, something held between his fingers.

Colt knocked lightly on the door and pushed it open. Michael looked up, holding the ring to the light. He handed it over to Colt and then glanced past him to Lexi, smiling too much as if he'd planned for the two of them to be together.

"It isn't much of a ring for an heirloom, is it?" Colt held the tiny band, gold with a quarter-carat diamond.

Michael shrugged. "It isn't big, but it means a

lot to the Logan family. It's a tradition that started with William Logan and Emmeline Carter, something like six generations back."

"I guess it didn't hold some lucky power, did it?" Colt gave the ring another look and shook his head.

"What do you mean by that?" Lexi slid into the room. He'd forgotten that she had followed him.

"I mean, the ring is an heirloom, but it doesn't guarantee a lasting marriage or happiness."

"That's cold." Lexi's chin went up a notch and her eyes narrowed. "It isn't about the ring making a marriage work. It's about family, and history, and people who were willing to work hard to make their lives something worthwhile that their children can look up to, and model their own lives after."

Colt held on to his serious demeanor, which wasn't easy in light of her foot-stomping anger. She was downright beautiful when she was mad.

And she was still dreaming of happy-ever-after. As if life was some kind of fairy tale. He had been her handsome prince, taking her out of the castle tower she'd been raised in to a life of happiness in a village with people who loved her.

He had been more than happy to play the role of prince to her princess in a tower. But then he had realized he couldn't slay all of the evil dragons. And he couldn't stick her back in the tower.

She cleared her throat, brows arching and

a ringless hand pushing back the curtain of brown hair.

"You're right, Lex. I'm sorry." He reached, but then lowered his hand. He wouldn't touch her, wouldn't brush that angry look off her face with a touch of his hand on her cheek.

"I called Jesse to let him know about the ring." Michael interrupted what could have been a tense moment. Wisely interrupted, Colt thought.

"I'll take it out there and let him see it." Colt held the ring up again. "I just don't know…"

"Why anyone would put the real ring in a box," Lexi finished for him.

He tried not to remember back to when they'd been together. At night they'd curled on the sofa together, discussing cases, hers and his. More often than not, those late-night conversations had helped them find answers they hadn't seen on their own.

It had been easy to talk about cases. Not as easy to talk about their marriage and why it wasn't working. He hadn't wanted to look that deeply inside himself.

The thought shook him a little, because he hadn't realized that before. He looked up, meeting Lexi's blue gaze, her soft smile.

"I think it probably isn't the Logan ring," Michael interjected.

"I'll take it out to him anyway. If it isn't the

real ring, then we'll have to solve the mystery of who and why." He slipped the ring into his shirt pocket.

Lexi's eyes lit with delight. She loved a mystery. "Can I go with you?"

At least he had agreed to let her tag along. Lexi waited for Colt to speak, but he was busy driving—busy thinking. His new patrol car was a Jeep, and it still had that new-car smell. She leaned back in the seat and had to admit it felt better than the old sedan. But what a way to get a new car, having the other totaled in a tornado. A tree had blown down and landed on it.

She didn't like to think of that day, or of how close they'd come to being seriously injured. Or worse. Jesse Logan's wife, Marie, hadn't survived the storm. And now he had three tiny babies to raise alone.

"Why the look?" Colt's words pulled her back to the moment.

"What look?"

"The dark look, the one that says you're thinking of something serious."

"The storm. I was thinking of how close I came to losing…" *You.* But she couldn't finish it, because that would refer to the dissolution of their marriage.

"I'm still here."

He had to know what she was thinking. He smiled, a halfway smile, flashing white teeth and dimples. But the smile was for her. It didn't reach his eyes.

"Yes, you're here." But not in her life, not really. She'd already lost him.

She sighed and looked out the window. They were getting close to the Logan ranch. She could see the roof of the house. It was a beautiful place, tall and stately, but welcoming.

"That day after the tornado, driving out here was the longest ride of my life," Colt shared. His voice was husky and all male, broken with emotion. "There's no easy way to tell someone that their spouse is dead. The person they leaned on—planned to spend their life with—is gone."

Lexi shivered and pushed the vent to the side, because she knew the memories that night must have evoked for him. He had been the one to tell Gavin's wife that her husband had been killed. He had stood in her doorway and watched her fall apart as their children stood in the background.

He had cried in Lexi's arms when he came home. He had shared the story, the grief in Gavin's wife's eyes, the tears of the children. And then Colt had retreated into some strange shell where he didn't share, not after that night.

He had blocked her from his life. She knew he

had meant it as a way to protect her. Or maybe himself. And she'd allowed it to an extent. She thought maybe she hadn't fought hard enough to keep their marriage alive. Maybe she had pushed him away, too, because she hadn't wanted to be the wife that lost her husband?

She glanced sideways, and he was staring straight ahead.

"Colt, we don't have to handle everything alone."

He nodded but didn't look at her. "I know that, Lex. I know that we can have faith."

She sighed and waited, wanting him to say that he had faith. But he didn't say it, because he couldn't. Faith was inside him somewhere, she knew it was. It had been planted there years ago, by a Sunday school teacher and his parents. He'd lost his way, but she was praying he'd find it again.

"Lex, why don't you move on?"

"Leave High Plains." She knew that wasn't what he meant.

"No, and you know better. Find someone to marry, someone who will give you that family you want and the home you've always dreamed of."

"Oh, that kind of moving on." She closed her eyes. "Is it that easy, Colt, to just forget someone and move on? Do you think I'm going to pick out a new man to replace you, just to have my happy-ever-after and a few kids?"

He didn't answer. She'd known he wouldn't, because he was honest, and he couldn't tell her it was easy. So instead he said nothing.

And she wouldn't tell him that she had tried moving on.

"Colt, I don't really understand what happened between us, or why you walked away from me. Sometimes I wonder if I did something wrong. I should have tried harder to work things out."

"No, Lexi, don't ever think that it was you. It was me. It was—" he glanced at her and then back to the road "—it was me, and my own…"

"Fear?"

He didn't answer.

Colt slowed as they neared the driveway to the Logan home. He couldn't answer Lexi. He hadn't moved on, because he still loved her. He loved her so much it was like a wound that wouldn't heal.

He wondered if Jesse Logan was still reeling with that same kind of pain. Or was Jesse's pain more about betrayal, because the night of the storm Marie had left him a Dear John letter and walked away from their lives together and her triplets?

People in town wondered if it was depression, postpartum, or something she had dealt with alone, not telling the people who cared about her.

Her life was cut short by the tornado. Jesse and

Marie would never have a chance to talk, to work things out. How many times had he thought of that over the last eight weeks? Too many to count.

What if it had been Lexi who had died in the tornado?

He shoved the thoughts aside and reached to turn up the radio. A love song blasted from the country station. *Every light in the house is on...* Some poor guy, waiting for a woman to come back to him. Colt turned the radio off and heard Lexi chuckle.

"What's so funny?"

"You. You're like a bear with a thorn in his paw. You're wounded and in pain, but you're not going to let anyone close enough to help."

"Nice."

"I'm a doctor. I can help."

"Amputation?" He smiled again, because that's what she did for him. She always made him smile. Accidents on the highway, helping family services remove abused children from homes, domestic violence...the realities of his job, and she'd always found a way to lighten the load.

"Thanks, Lex."

"Don't mention it. And please, don't give up."

"Yeah, okay."

"That's optimistic."

He shot her a look and she shrugged.

"'Yeah, okay'?" she repeated, deepening her voice to imitate him. He laughed again.

"I sound that happy?"

"No, not even close. I made you sound better than you are."

"I'll work on it." He braked to a stop in front of the house. "Man, I don't want to do this."

"He's going to tell you it's the wrong ring."

She had that tilt to her chin, the one that said she was right and she knew it. He smiled and pushed his door open. "You're probably right, but I want to make sure."

"And then what?" She was out and at his side as they walked up the wide steps to the front door.

"I'll find out who put it in there and why. Or maybe we've got it all wrong and the person who put it in the box didn't intend to make us think it was the Logan ring. It could just be a lost ring that was found."

"I like the mystery better. It adds suspense."

Colt laughed and slid an arm around her waist, just for a moment, just long enough to pull her close and kiss the side of her head, to smell the herbal scent of shampoo.

He knocked on the door and in a moment it was opened by Jesse.

"Sorry to bother you, Jess." Colt slid the ring

out of his pocket. At least this time it wasn't the worst news he could give another man.

"No problem, Colt. I'm glad you called and caught me at home."

"Here it is." Colt handed Jesse Logan the ring. Jesse motioned them inside and then he paused and did a double take. Colt followed his gaze to Lexi.

"I didn't realize that was you, Lexi." Jesse held his hand out and took Lexi's for a moment. And Colt wanted to pull her hand loose.

That didn't make sense. He let it go, because it was a greeting, nothing more, and he wasn't a jealous teenager.

"I was at the church when they found the ring," Lexi explained, still standing at Colt's side. "Colt let me ride out with him."

"Would the two of you like a glass of tea?" Jesse held the ring up to the sunlight that streamed through the window.

"No, thanks. We wanted to let you see the ring and then we need to head back to town. Lexi probably has strays to rescue and I need to get some paperwork done."

Jesse nodded and then he handed the ring back to Colt. "It isn't the ring."

"I didn't think it was." Colt moved to the side as Lexi's elbow shot out. "We didn't think it was."

"I'm starting to think we won't find it." Jesse

brushed a hand through his hair. "It's just hard to imagine it being gone, and that I won't be able to pass it on to my daughter. All of these years, that one ring has been in our family. And in one day, it was all taken away."

His wife, the ring, his dreams for his family. Colt didn't know what to say.

"We're going to find it," Lexi piped in, all faith and sunshine. Colt wanted to bring her down to earth, but he couldn't.

He wouldn't do that. Instead his attention caught and held on the family portraits that covered the walls of the foyer. One portrait in particular, Jesse's brother Clay, caught his eye.

"Have you heard from Clay?" It made sense that this family tragedy would bring the lost Logan home. Wouldn't Clay want to be here for his brother?

"Not a word. Maya left the message and he answered that, I guess. But, well, you know he isn't spending too many dimes to call me."

"I'm sorry, Jesse. Let me know if there's anything I can do." Colt patted the other man on the shoulder and turned to the door, Lexi behind him.

Or he thought she was. He turned as she gave Jesse Logan a quick hug. "I'm praying for you and for the babies."

Jesse nodded and Lexi moved away. Colt

opened the door and she followed him out. She was praying, always praying. He knew she prayed for him, that he was safe.

"Let's go home, Lex." The words slipped out. He glanced away.

*Let's go home.* Lexi let the words play through her mind as they drove back to town. How many years had she spent at his side, hearing those words? Now, the words meant that he would drop her off at her home.

And it wasn't even a home now; it was a dozed-over hole in the ground. She didn't want to think of that, of what that empty space on her lot symbolized. She would rebuild.

But what was lost, was lost. Family photos, keepsakes from her marriage and her childhood, all gone.

Her eyes grew heavy and she leaned back, willing to take a short nap if it kept her from thinking too much. Sunshine warmed her face and she closed her eyes against its brilliance. Country music played on the radio. As the Jeep bounced along the country road, Colt sang along to a country ballad.

She opened her eyes as they pulled in the driveway of her clinic. It was her home now. She shared it with a pigmy goat, a dozen or so cats and dogs, someone's pet rabbit that had wandered into her yard and an owl that had a wounded wing.

It didn't always smell pleasant, but it was hers. Home sweet home. Colt lived on the outskirts of town in an old cottage that had once belonged to his grandmother.

Funny how things had changed. She was happy. Even without the dream life she had thought she wanted. Real faith had changed so much in her life. This new ingredient, she realized, was contentment.

"Lex, your front door is open a little. Do you think you didn't pull it closed?" Colt's question froze her heart.

"Of course I closed it." She was wide-awake now.

"Stay in the car." He was out, hand on his side, reaching for the weapon that wasn't there.

"Wait, I'm going with you." She grabbed her purse and hurried after him. He turned, shooting her that look that did nothing but make her want to go even more.

"Stay in the car. You don't know who is in there. Lexi, you have drugs in there that someone in need of a fix might try to steal. And if they need a fix, they're not going to be in a good mood."

"It's my house."

"I'm not your ex-husband right now—I'm a police officer. Stay put."

She obeyed, because he had that steely quality

to his voice that said he meant it. He wanted to keep her safe. She wished he could love her as much as he wanted to protect her.

"Okay, I'm staying."

He walked to the edge of the building and then down to the window. He peeked in and then went back, slipping through the door that wasn't latched. She knew she had locked that door. She never left without making sure all of the doors and windows were latched.

As she waited, she prayed, because she wanted him to be safe, and she wanted her animals safe. She tried to push aside the last conversation with her mother that had included the questions about her life, and why she wouldn't just come home.

Sometimes the idea of moving tempted her.

She moved closer to the door, because she couldn't stand there and wait. And then Colt was there, smiling a little. He motioned her inside.

"It isn't a thief." Colt pulled someone from the side of the door. "It's Tommy. I guess, in reality, he did break in, but he didn't steal anything."

"Tommy?" Lexi knelt in front of the boy. "What are you doing here?"

"Looking for Charlie. I followed Chico, because he used to play with me and Charlie. I thought maybe he'd know where my dog went to."

"Oh, honey, I wish I had your dog, but I don't.

And doesn't Mr. Garrison have a puppy for you at his house?"

He nodded his little tear-stained face, and Lexi cried with him, holding him close. His little body shook and sobs rolled out, harsh and uncontrolled. Her own tears were hot against her cheeks and she wished she could make it all better for him.

"That puppy isn't the same." The boy sobbed against her, his words coming out broken and full of grief. "I just want my dog Charlie back, because he was my best friend and no one has put him in the lost and found at the church."

"Honey, I don't think he would stay there. He'd come looking for you." She wiped his tears with her fingers. "But I do know that if he's out there somewhere, he's trying to get back to you. And if someone finds him, they'll bring him back."

"Do you think he will come home?"

Lexi pulled away, but still held on to slim little shoulders. He was a mess, this kid, always in trouble, always up to something. But Lexi knew that he just wanted love. He wanted to belong to someone and something. She swallowed and nodded to answer his question.

"Dogs are smart, Tommy. Sometimes they go miles and miles to get home. I had one dog that I gave to a family that lived ten miles from High

Plains. That silly dog liked it here so much, he walked all the way back."

"I sure hope that Charlie is that smart." Tommy sniffled. "But I don't know. He never did act too smart."

"Of course he was smart, Tommy." Colt patted the boy's back. "That day of the tornado, he was barking at you, trying to warn you. He's a smart dog."

Tommy looked up, nodding and wiping his nose and then his eyes with his hand. Lexi bit down on her lip and hid her smile. "Let's get you a tissue and then we can call for someone to pick you up. I think Mr. Garrison is going to be very worried about you."

Because the child finally had someone who wanted to always be in his life. And she was thinking about lyrics of a song that said she would find better love, stronger than it ever was.

Lexi looked at Colt. He had his cell phone out and was dialing. He had been her someone, the person who she thought would always be in her life. She prayed little Tommy wouldn't be let down.

## Chapter Four

The room was still bathed in gray early-morning light when Lexi woke up the next morning. It was too early to get up, and she hadn't gotten much sleep, not with the Tommy incident replaying in her mind all night, along with the memory of Colt singing along with the car radio. She had dreamed about it, and her heart ached with a fresh pain, when only a week earlier she had thought maybe, just maybe, she was moving on.

She didn't know how a couple went from forever to goodbye, without looking back.

Groggy and grouchy, she started a pot of coffee and grabbed a bag of cat food out of the closet. The kittens gathered around the cage door and she had to push past them to put food in their dish. She rubbed the head of a gray tabby and he bit at her fingers.

"Oh, that's real nice. Biting the hand that feeds you." She picked him up and held him close. "I need to find homes for you guys. Maybe this idea of Michael's will work and we'll be able to match pets with people."

The phone rang. She reached for it as she poured herself a cup of coffee, spilling a little on the counter and wiping it up with a paper towel.

"Doc, this is Hammer. I've got a cow out here that is just about down. Do you think you could run by and check on her?"

"Sure I can. It'll be an hour or so. I left my truck at the church yesterday."

"Yep, some of the fellers said they saw you leaving town with the chief yesterday."

A question in his voice and she wasn't about to answer those questions. But then again, she wasn't going to let gossip start a relationship that had ended a couple of years ago.

"We ran out to visit Jesse Logan."

"Gotcha. Well, anyway, if you don't mind checking the cow. Oh, Doc, there was a dog running the far side of my field yesterday. We couldn't catch up with it, but one of my guys thought it might be Tommy's dog Charlie. I hope he ain't running cows."

"I don't think he'd be running cows. I think he'd

be trying to make his way home to Tommy. I'll keep an eye out as I drive."

"Okay, thanks."

"Hammer, don't mention to the little boy that you thought it was his dog. We don't want to get his hopes up."

"Sure thing, Doc. See ya later."

Lexi poured her coffee from her ceramic mug, with the picture of a Labrador, to a thermal mug and grabbed a breakfast bar. So much for taking it easy this morning. On her way out the door, she grabbed antibiotics from the fridge and shoved them into her black bag.

It was a cool fall morning and the sun was burning off the gray haze. Lexi loved Kansas in autumn. She loved the smell of drying grass, autumn flowers and the crispness of the air.

As she walked down the sidewalk, past buildings that were still standing, and some that would never stand again, she thought about how this fall was different than last. Last year she'd still been grieving her lost marriage. Today she was grieving the loss of her town, her home and friends who had moved away.

But she had hope. She had a strong feeling that God was doing something. She couldn't see it, but she could feel it in her heart, where it felt a little like a lighter step and an easier smile.

"Hey, Doc Ridgeway." A woman's voice called from the door of the city hall. "Come back here."

Lexi turned and smiled at Gloria Dawson, the spitfire of a mayor that kept High Plains running smoothly. And sometimes caused an uproar over some new city policy. Those policies were usually needed, but hard for a small town to adjust to.

"How can I help you, Mayor?"

"You can help me by clearing farm animals out of your lot."

"Farm animals?" Lexi pulled the strap of her bag onto her shoulder as it slid down her arm. "What do you mean?"

"You have goats and chickens in the pens outside of your office."

"They're refugees, Mayor. They don't have anywhere to go."

"I know that, but you know the ordinances. I don't want to make this hard on you, because you're helping out." Gloria sighed. "I'm stuck between a rock and a hard place, Lexi. But you have to do something before Hank files a complaint against you."

Hank Farris, the local cranky guy. Lexi made a face and Gloria smiled. "You know I can't help this, Lexi."

"I know you can't. But there has to be something we can do. This is temporary. It isn't like I'm raising cattle in my front yard."

"I know that. But find homes for them as soon as you can."

"We're hoping to adopt some of them out at the church fellowship. Tell Hank I'll bring him eggs from the chickens if he'll give me a break."

"I think he's allergic."

Gloria saluted and headed back into the city hall. Main Street. Lexi sighed as she turned that corner and her heart ached for the business owners who had lost so much. More than insurance would cover. The General Store was still a mess of bricks and glass. They were waiting for insurance to pay so they could hire someone to clean it up.

That was happening all over town. People were ready to get their lives back in order, their homes put back together, but they couldn't. Some insurance companies had paid quickly, others had loopholes.

Lexi crossed the street that still wasn't as busy as it had been two months earlier. She pulled her keys out of her pocket and unlocked her truck. She set her bag in the passenger seat and then went to check supplies in the back of her truck.

A car pulled in behind her. She turned and her heart caught a little. The Jeep engine purred smoothly, and Colt waved and then hopped out. Chico was in the backseat, his Labrador tail wagging so hard she could hear it pounding the door panel.

"Where are you off to?" Colt walked around to where she stood. And she couldn't look away because he smiled that way he did, and she remembered how it felt to be held by him.

When she looked at him, she thought of the year they had dated, when for the first time in her life, she had felt as if someone would always be there for her. She had been so lonely until she met him.

He had brought her here, to High Plains, to his family. She missed him, but she was no longer that searching, lonely kid.

That thought made her hold her chin a little higher as she answered.

"Hammer has a cow that's down. What about you?"

"I got a call. Some people think they remember seeing a woman with a little girl that matches Kasey's description. I'm hoping it will lead somewhere." Rather than the endless, nowhere leads Lexi knew he'd already had. "I'm hoping they have a little more to share."

"I'll be praying…."

He smiled an easy smile. "I know you will be."

"Colt." She swallowed because words weren't always as easily said as thought. She could go over this a million times in her mind, but to actually put it into words, it felt like skydiving for the first time. "Colt, I miss you."

His smile dissolved. "Lexi, don't do this."

"I'm sorry, but I wanted you to know." She shrugged and walked away because he didn't want to hear, and she wouldn't push.

She missed him. As Colt drove north, that's all he could think about. He could only picture the look on her face as the wind lifted brown hair, and her eyes glistened. There were so many reasons why her missing him was a mistake. And more reasons why he couldn't tell her that she was the last thing he thought about when he went to sleep at night, and the first thing he thought about each morning when he woke up.

That must qualify as missing her, too.

But he knew they couldn't go back. He couldn't go back to worrying that something would happen to him, and that she'd be the one left alone. He couldn't think about starting a family when something like that could happen.

He could think about all the ways he'd let her down, though. And that helped him to remember why missing her was better than hurting her.

Almost an hour after leaving High Plains he pulled up to a farmhouse that had seen better days. The paint was weathered and the barn was falling in. An old tractor was parked at the back of the house, the tires flat and weeds growing up through the engine. A dog as old as the tractor barked from the front porch.

Colt felt a little uneasy as he got out of the Jeep. His hand moved to his sidearm, and then he walked up to the front door. The dog sniffed his leg and walked away, uninterested.

The front door opened and an older woman in a housedress peeked out at him. "You that law officer from High Plains."

"Yes. ma'am, I am."

"Come on in."

Colt took off his hat and followed her inside. She pointed to a floral sofa covered in plastic. He sat down. "You said you have information about the little girl we have in High Plains."

"I don't know how much it'll help you." She sat in a fabric-covered rocking chair that squeaked when she rocked. "But there's a reward, right?"

Colt let out a sigh and nodded. "For information leading to the parents, yes. Or if you can positively identify the child."

"I can't identify her, but I think I saw her with her mom. The day before the tornado a woman came through this area. She had a little girl with her."

"Did you talk to her?"

"Not much. She was at the store in town. She

seemed like she didn't want to stay around long. Said she was passing through."

"If I show you five pictures of little girls, do you think you can pick her picture?"

She shrugged. "I can try."

Colt opened the plastic folder and produced the pictures for the woman to look at. She lifted glasses that hung from a chain around her neck. She shook her head as she stared at the pictures.

"It was so long ago now." She shook her head again and let the glasses drop back to her chest. "Nope, I don't recognize her. It could be that one on the far right, but I'm not sure."

It was Kasey. Colt nodded. He pulled money out of his pocket and handed it to her. "Thank you. That isn't reward money, it's just to help you out a little."

"Bless you. I'm real sorry that I wasted your time. But bless you for caring for an old widow. You're a good Christian boy." Her eyes watered as she pushed herself out of the chair. "I do hope you find her momma."

"Me, too." But his heart ached a little at the thought. If he found Kasey's mother, Nicki Appleton's heart would be broken.

Following him to the door, she reminded him of his grandmother in her housedress and orthopedic shoes. As he walked down the crumbling steps, he fought back memories of his grandmother singing in church, and how he had always felt like a fraud because everyone sang along but him.

He had spent a lot of years angry at God, and sometimes angry at his family for not losing faith. They had nearly lost everything else. But faith was the one thing they always had a lot of.

Now, he looked back and wondered how he resented the thing that kept them together, that kept them smiling and hoping for better days. It seemed silly now, to think that he resented the faith that had made his family whole and happy, and his childhood one of laughter and play.

His parents had never given up. And his grandmother had always sung "Amazing Grace" as if it meant everything.

He drove from the old farmhouse to the Waters cottages. He was pulling down the narrow drive to the spot where Kasey had been found when he heard a vehicle downshift. He turned and watched as Lexi's truck turned and eased down the drive to park behind his.

Lately it seemed as if she was everywhere. He knew what his mom would say about that. She'd say something like maybe it was God showing him the right path.

More than likely it was just because they lived in a small town and people bumped into each other nearly every day.

His thoughts returned to the fact that he hadn't been out to see his parents for a couple of weeks. He needed to get back out there, soon. But at the moment, Lexi was walking toward him, her smile a little hesitant.

"What are you doing out here?" He pulled sunglasses out of his pocket and put them on.

"A sick cow and a horse with thrush." She shrugged and looked away from him. "What about you? How did your meeting go?"

"An older woman that needed reward money. But I think she might have actually seen Kasey."

"So you're here to…what?"

"Look for something that I'm missing." He glanced away from her, thinking about that, about missing something. "There has to be something here that I haven't found, or seen. She was here, so maybe there's something else."

"Or maybe not. Maybe she was dropped here by the tornado? Maybe it carried her a short distance? What if her mom left her here to run into town, left her alone?"

He started walking toward the area where Greg Garrison had found Kasey. Lexi, in work boots, jeans and a T-shirt, walked along next to him. Their fingers touched, but he didn't take hold of her hand. She didn't look at him.

"Colt, there might not be anything here."

He knew what she meant. She knew that sometimes a case got hold of him and he couldn't let go. He had spent days combing the side of the road where Gavin had been shot and weeks searching for the shooter. He'd caught him, too. He was going to find out what happened to Kasey's mother.

"Colt, don't let this eat away at you." Lexi's fingers touched his again.

"Are you telling me to let it go?"

"No, I'm not. I'm saying, don't…" She smiled. "Don't forget I'm praying."

Like his mother, always praying. He smiled at her, at the wistful look in her eyes, because this faith stuff was real to her. It was what she'd been looking for when she faithfully attended church each Sunday. His leaving had taken her to this place, where it was real.

"Could you pray that God would show me what I'm missing?"

"I'll pray you'll see what you're missing." She kissed his cheek and walked away.

He brushed a hand through his hair and shook his head a little. He knew exactly what he was missing. He watched her get in the Ford truck and drive away.

Lexi drove back to town with the radio cranked and the windows open, letting cool air blow through the cab of the truck. She called herself lots of names for stopping when she saw Colt. It was as if she couldn't help herself. He was such a part of her heart, but she really had thought that she was moving on.

The tornado had changed more than the landscape.

It had changed how she felt. Or maybe just reminded her how it felt to be in his arms.

Her cell phone rang. She answered and cringed a little when she realized it was the number of the fellowship director for singles at High Plains Community Church. She had attended a few functions, gotten matched up on a few blind dates, and now they thought she was on the market.

"Vera, how can I help you?" Lexi hit her turn signal and pulled onto the quiet street just off Main Street that led to her veterinary clinic, and what had once been her house.

"We're having an impromptu meeting tonight." Vera chewed gum, even on the phone. "We'd love for you to bring some of that great chicken casserole I know you have in the freezer."

"I don't know, Vera, I'm really beat." And that wasn't a lie. For the last five miles she'd been yawning nonstop.

"I know you are, honey. But we're making up posters for nearby towns. We've finished Kasey posters and we're going to make more for Tommy's dog. I know it's been eight weeks, but there's still hope."

"Yes, there's hope." But the hope was dwindling. Lexi couldn't bring herself to say that. She remembered her own lost dog when she was a kid. She'd made posters for months, hanging them all over their neighborhood. Her parents had been too busy, so she had called the humane society herself.

"So, you'll be there?"

For Tommy and his dog. "Yes, I'll be there."

She would have to take a quick shower, stick the casserole in the microwave and feed her animals. She was exhausted thinking about it, about rushing around when she only wanted a cup of coffee and a few minutes sitting outside by herself.

When she pulled up to the church an hour later it looked as if a good crowd had gathered. And Lexi didn't want a big crowd, not tonight when her heart was feeling a little bruised by everything going on.

She could put it down to the tornado, the damage to the town, the loss of her house, Tommy and his dog and Kasey. It had a lot to do with Colt.

But tonight was a good night for getting her mind off him. Her phone rang and she answered it.

"It's me." Jill.

"Are you watching out the window to see if I'll leave?"

"No, of course not."

"Yes, you are. And I'm not leaving. I'm going to come in there, get pushed at the pick-of-the-month and maybe even accept when he asks me to go out."

"Whatever." Jill laughed, real and contagious.

"I mean it." Lexi got out of her truck, still on the phone. Jill opened the door, waiting for her.

"Of course you do. Hey, do you know the guy that just pulled in?"

Lexi glanced back at the car pulling in next to hers. "He doesn't belong here."

"He can't come to church?"

"He can come to church, but he doesn't attend functions like this. He's too cool." Lexi had reached the door and clicked off her phone. Jill hugged her. "And if I have to watch single women fawn all over him, I'm leaving."

"Because you care?" Jill hugged her again and waved at Colt.

"No, I don't care. But what gives. You'd better tell me before he gets up here and we can't talk."

"I think he's here to give us information for the posters. That's all."

Lexi shook her head and pinched Jill's arm. "That's a lie. And you're in church."

"It is not a lie, not completely." Jill pulled Lexi to the corner of the vestibule, closing the door behind them. "He's here because people are starting to get the idea that the two of you need to get back together."

Lexi swallowed hard and tried to breathe, but it hurt. "This can't be happening."

"Sorry, but it is."

"I should go." But the door opened and Colt walked in, still wearing his dark jeans and the T-shirt that said Police in big white letters.

She remembered when he had been a lanky farm kid, going to college. Now he was filled out in all the right places and still as confident as ever. He walked with purpose, steady and lethal. His smile was just as lethal. It made her knees weak.

Or maybe she had a virus. She had been around some runny-nosed kids lately. That could be it. And she hadn't eaten yet. So maybe her blood-sugar levels were low. That would explain the way her heart raced a little and her skin felt a little sweaty and clammy at the same time.

"You two look like you're up to something." He took off the cowboy hat that was a part of his uniform and ran fingers through slightly shaggy sun-bleached hair.

"You need a haircut," Lexi shot back.

"I agree. So, do you agree that the two of you are acting like you're up to something?"

Jill laughed, an easy, unaffected laugh. "Honey,

we're not the ones up to something. Come on in, though."

"I have the information you need." Colt handed it to Jill. "But I'm not sure if more posters will do the trick."

"You never know." Jill motioned him inside. "Stay and help us?"

"Can't." He looked a little relieved by that. "I have a city council meeting."

"Lucky you." Lexi glanced into the fellowship hall of the church and realized the odds were good for the men. Lots of lonely, single women and five men.

"You'll have a good time." Colt leaned, sniffing the casserole that she still held. "Smells good."

"You don't want to stay and eat?" she offered.

"Not on your life, sweetheart."

## Chapter Five

Colt sat at the back of the meeting room attached to the fire department waiting for his turn to speak. The voices droned and he didn't pay much attention to the topics. Someone's lawn wasn't mowed, they needed a new mower and the city clerk had requested a raise.

Headlights flashed around the corner. Finally, something to catch his attention. He watched, waiting to see who it was. And it was Lexi. He had called her as soon as he got to the meeting, to let her know that her name wasn't on the agenda, but Hank Farris had brought up her animals and planned on trying to sneak the discussion into the meeting. He thought Lexi should try to make the meeting. She slowed as she passed, and then he saw her brake lights reflected in the window of the door.

"Chief, did you hear that question?" Mayor

Dawson asked, her voice echoed off the bare walls of the room. "Jeremy French wants to know if you're aware of those boys that have been scavenging through some of the homes."

"We're aware, but we need for someone to do more than point fingers. We need a call during the actual scavenging, or the real identities of those involved. I've talked to some boys, but none of them are talking or taking responsibility for the thefts."

Jeremy grunted and looked none too pleased. The door behind Colt opened, bringing in cool air and the light floral of Lexi's perfume. He turned, and she smiled an uneasy smile. He pointed to the chair next to his. The chair she used to sit in during every city council meeting. Until they separated.

Since then the chair had been empty.

"How was church?" he whispered as she sat down.

"Fun." She smiled forward, and he turned his attention back to the meeting and to Mayor Dawson, eyebrows raised in question.

"Are you still with us, Chief?" Gloria Dawson smiled a little too big. "We were talking about thieves."

"I'm investigating that problem, Mayor. I promise we're not ignoring it."

"Then we'll move on. Hank Farris is here because he has a minor issue in his neighborhood.

Doc, since you're here, maybe we could talk about that ark of yours." Mayor Dawson pointed the gavel in Lexi's direction.

Colt shook his head. "With all due respect, Mayor, that isn't on the agenda. We have more important things to discuss, like a grant to try and get another warning siren."

"Chief, I'm not going to put up with farm animals in town just because your ex-wife is the one with the animals." Hank stood up, his face shadowed with whiskers and his hands hitched in his bib overalls.

"Mr. Farris, you know that the animals are there temporarily. I'm finding homes for them." She smiled, and Colt wondered how Hank couldn't cave under that look of hers. And the crusty old guy did look like someone about to give in.

"I'm tired of the noise," he grumbled before sitting down.

Colt stood up. "Hank, she'll find homes for the farm animals by the end of the month. Does that work?"

"It works."

"Good, then let's get back to what is on the agenda. Storm sirens. I'd like to have two, if we could. There are people in town who don't hear the one siren that we have."

"Chief, I am aware of that complaint, and we're

going to do our best. We have a limited amount of money…."

"And we need to put the money we have toward a siren," Colt insisted. "Mayor, I'm writing the grant but it might not be enough for two sirens. I'd like for the city to plan on putting some money toward this, as I believe it is a very important safety issue."

"I agree," one of the council members interjected. "I can hear that siren if I'm outside, but chances are, I'm not going to be outside waiting to hear the siren."

The mayor pounded her gavel on the card table that they set up for meetings. "Fine, we'll table this, and at the next meeting I'll let you know what we have available, and you'll have that grant written."

Colt smiled. "Thank you, Mayor."

"Good. So, let's adjourn this meeting," Henry Parker grumbled. "I'm about sick of hearing about overgrown lawns and too many pets."

Colt waited for the meeting to be adjourned and then he stood up, motioning Lexi outside ahead of him. She pulled on her jacket as they walked and then pulled her hair loose from the collar.

He wanted to help, because there were still strands under the collar of her jacket. He pushed his hands into his pockets and followed her to her truck. And his mind took another turn, back to the cottages that afternoon and a scrap of material that might mean something. Or maybe wouldn't.

It could be a lead, something that pointed in the direction of Kasey's mother. He had it in a bag in his office, because he wasn't ready to share it, not yet. He didn't want to stir speculation or start rumors.

"Hey, for five minutes, could you listen to me?"

He looked up from the sidewalk and met blue eyes that were as familiar as the sky. He shrugged, unsure of what he'd done or what she wanted from him.

He was clueless. It was part of being a man, his mom had always told him. Maybe she was wrong. Maybe some men did get it, and weren't clueless.

"I'm sorry?"

"I was asking you a question." She pulled the key out of her purse and hit the remote to unlock the door of her truck.

"Sorry, I was thinking."

"About?" she prodded, standing next to him, buttoning her jacket because the wind was brisk, and it smelled a lot as if it might rain.

"Kasey, Tommy's dog, the ring and working on the Old Town Hall tomorrow. Plus, I need to go out and help my folks vaccinate some calves." He shook his head. "And Walter's house has a hole in the roof."

"You're always busy, Colt."

"I know, Lex. I know." Part of the wedge that had driven them apart, his preoccupation with work.

"I only want a few minutes of your time, a few minutes when I feel like you're really listening to me."

"I'm sorry." And he really was.

"Don't worry about it. But, Colt, someday, if someone comes into your life, give her your time. Don't make her feel like she comes second to everything and everyone else."

He closed his eyes for a brief second and this time when he whispered that he was sorry, it meant more than just the words that he had uttered too many times. He opened his eyes and she was watching him.

"I forgive you." She touched his cheek, and he turned into the gesture, grazing the palm of her hands with a kiss.

Lexi's heart ached as Colt's lips touched her hand. She pulled back, crossing her arms in front of her and unsure of how to escape what was happening.

"How about a cup of coffee?" He said it softly, tempting her.

"Coffee?" She glanced at her watch. "It's nearly ten o'clock."

"Decaf?"

"Tastes horrible. Do you have chamomile tea? I could use something that will help me sleep."

"I actually do."

What was she thinking? This would only hurt later. It felt a lot as if it might hurt now, and she wouldn't even have to wait until later. But Colt's eyes connected with hers and didn't waver, and she was so tired of missing him. She was tired of listening to Glenn Barker as he tried to sell her on the benefit of whole life insurance, as well as a date with him.

Not that Glenn was a bad guy. But her heart couldn't let go of a memory, or what had once been. Her heart still ached for the man standing in front of her, because she had never stopped loving him.

She had gotten tired of being left alone while everyone and everything else took top priority. How could she have children with a man that worked twenty-four-hour shifts and never turned off his cell phone?

She didn't want that for her children, a childhood that mimicked her own. She wanted something different, a family that spent time together.

He hadn't always been that way, putting his job first. Losing Gavin had done that to him. It had changed them both, because after Gavin's death, Lexi had been afraid to let Colt leave for work.

Too bad she hadn't discovered the peace that comes from having faith until after their divorce.

"It's only a cup of tea, Lex," he teased, and she thought he might reach for her hand. He didn't.

A cup of tea, and maybe they could really talk. They hadn't done much of that in the last year of their marriage. When she had tried, he had walked out, unable to hear that they were falling apart.

Or unwilling to fix it.

"A cup of tea." She nodded in agreement. "I'll follow you."

She got into her truck and started it, still telling herself she should go home. She shouldn't let herself fall back into this, into needing him this much.

Her hand settled on her phone, and she almost dialed his number, nearly told him that this was a bad idea. But instead she followed him to his house, pulling into the driveway of the one-bedroom cottage right behind him.

When he got out, she waited, still having a serious talk with herself about the danger involved in having tea with Colt. Her mind took a trip back to college and to having him in her life, holding her hand, being there for her every day. He had made her laugh. He had been the first person to make her feel as if she wasn't alone.

She had known, even then, that he had this insane sense of responsibility. She had known then that he had a past, ghosts of some kind that he didn't share. But that injured part of him had drawn her, too. He was everything she wanted. He had grown up in a real family, with laughter and Sunday dinners. He was strong and capable. He was tender and hurting.

He had loved her. She could see in his eyes that the feelings weren't gone. That made losing him hurt all the more.

It made her want to work this out—to talk—even more. And that's why she took the keys from the ignition and smiled through the closed window of her truck.

He opened her truck door and she stepped out, not sure what to say or how to say it. His house, a small cottage, dark without a security light and no porch light, sat to the left of the driveway. Chico ran out from behind the house, pounding the ground like a bull on the rampage.

"Chico, stay down," Colt ordered and the dog slowed to a lumbering pace, but his panting tongue was out, ready to show them love.

"He's a mess." Lexi finally spoke, but it took a lot to get the words out. Her gaze shot past Colt and the dog to the house.

"Tea, Lexi, just tea. It's been a long day. We

could both use a friend who understands, and who isn't trying to fix us up with someone else."

"I thought you were dating." She bit down on her lip after the words slipped out. She didn't want to be catty.

"Maybe three times in the last year."

"Jackie Gardner."

He nodded. "She teaches kindergarten now, and I think she's dating the new fifth-grade teacher. She told me I'm obsessed with my job."

"Hmm, imagine that." Lexi smiled and waited for Colt to see the humor in the comment. He smiled a little and took hold of her hand.

He fished the key out of his pocket with his left hand and let go of her hand long enough to unlock the front door. "Have a seat, and I'll get the water on."

"Out here." She pointed to the chairs on the front porch. She couldn't go inside. "I'll wait for you."

He shrugged. "Suit yourself."

Lexi stood at the edge of the porch and watched as Colt walked into the house. Lights came on. She could hear the radio through the opened window and Colt talking to Chico, because the dog had followed him.

It was time for her to get a new dog of her own. Obviously Chico wasn't coming back. It had been two years.

She sat on the edge of one of the wicker chairs and leaned forward, feeling a little cool in the crisp autumn night. Somewhere an owl screeched and a car horn honked. Through the open window she could hear Colt singing along, off-key and loud, to George Strait as he banged around in the kitchen.

The screen door creaked. Lexi watched as Chico worked it open with his nose and then slid through the opening. The door banged shut and he hurried to her side.

"Hey, buddy." She rubbed his ears and he pushed closer with a toy.

She took the slobbery tennis ball from his mouth and gave it a toss. The dog lumbered into the yard, sniffing in the general direction of the ball until he found it. He walked back to her, but this time he dropped the ball and sat down.

"Want me to throw it again?" She reached for it, but the dog grabbed it first and trotted off.

"There's something wrong with a Lab that doesn't like to play fetch." Colt pushed the door open with his shoulder and joined her, holding out one of the cups he carried.

He sat in the chair next to hers, and Lexi knew they wouldn't talk. She knew they would have tea and she would leave, and they would be right where they left off—not dealing with the marriage that had come unraveled.

She sipped the chamomile, knowing that within thirty minutes it would have her drowsy and ready for bed. But it tasted good, with just the right amount of sugar.

"Did I get it right?" Colt asked.

"Perfect." She sipped again. Chico was back, without the tennis ball. He'd probably buried it. That's what he did with things that they played with. When he was done playing their people games, he buried the toys.

"Crazy dog."

She nodded and leaned back, feeling a little more relaxed. Probably thanks to the tea and to the cool night air.

"Colt, I'm not sure why I'm here. We have to figure this out."

"I know."

"I miss you, but I'm not willing to do this again." Falling apart because they couldn't communicate and because they were both afraid. "I'm not afraid anymore."

"I'm glad." He sighed, and she knew he was remembering the night she called his cell phone twenty times because he wasn't answering, and she didn't know that he was in a dead spot, without a signal. She had worried that something had happened to him.

"A lot has changed."

"We've changed."

"We're older and wiser." She smiled over the brim of her cup and took a drink.

"I'm not sure about the wiser stuff. But, Lexi, my job hasn't changed. I know you have faith, but I'm still struggling with that. I still think about finding Gavin. I still think about his wife and kids, and how it felt to tell them. I think about how it would be for my own wife and kids to get that news."

Her world crumbled a little because his pain matched hers, and yet they were dealing with it alone. She set her cup down on the table next to the chair and turned. He looked as miserable as he sounded.

"Colt, that isn't going to happen."

"It could, Lex. It could. I know that High Plains is a safe place. I thought this county was safe, that we were protected from what happens in cities."

"And because of Gavin, you think you were wrong?" Pain mingled with anger, and she didn't know which to deal with. Anger seemed easier. "This isn't fair. I want to be understanding. But you took away my dreams, my future with the man I love."

"I did it to protect you." He stood up, his cup still in his hand.

"And yet, here I am." She stood up and walked toward him. "I'm here, Colt."

He set the cup down on the rail of the porch. Lexi waited, breathless. Her invitation was clear and she didn't have long to wait. His hands tangled in her hair and he drew her close, holding her near to him, so near she could feel his breath on her neck and hear the steady beat of his heart. His lips grazed her cheek and then her lips.

"I miss you." She whispered close to his ear and then his lips were on hers again.

"I know. Me, too."

Lexi wrapped her arms around his waist and he held her close. And she didn't want to leave. She didn't want to spend another night alone, with her husband a mile down the road with her dog. She didn't want to wake up alone, knowing he still loved her and she still loved him.

Chico ran up the steps and dropped a stick at their feet.

"Stupid dog, now he decides to play fetch." Colt's words were a little shaky.

And Lexi returned to reality, where her husband was no longer her husband. He had made a choice, to put his career first.

"I need to go." She grabbed her purse. "Thank you for the tea."

"Lexi, don't leave like this." Colt followed her down the stairs.

"There is no *leaving*, Colt. You already left, remember. This is just leftovers, and I don't want leftovers."

He reached for her hand and pulled her back. "I didn't mean to hurt you. I wanted to protect you. I wanted you to have everything."

"You were my everything. You were the person who made me smile. You helped me believe in myself. And then you took it all away because you decided it was too difficult."

His hand was still holding hers and he lifted it to kiss her palm. "I never meant to hurt you."

"But you did."

Colt watched her drive away. Chico stood next to him, pushing the stick against Colt's hand, asking to play. He reached down and ran his fingers through the soft fur at the dog's neck.

"I really messed things up, Chico."

A door slammed, the neighbor's porch light went on. "Colt, is that you out there?"

"It is, Jeremiah. Sorry if I was too noisy."

"You weren't noisy. Was that Lexi, leaving out here all mad?"

Colt groaned, quietly, and only Chico heard. The dog pushed a cold nose into his hand. Dog sympathy, just what he needed.

"Yes, it was Lexi."

"Thought so. You think you two kids might work it out?"

Work it out. That made it sound as if something disastrous had happened to their marriage. That was probably what people thought. But it hadn't been something disastrous. It had been a shift on his part, and at the moment it felt like a huge mistake.

"I doubt if we'll work it out, Jeremiah. We were just having a cup of tea."

"You gotta start somewhere, Colt. Sometimes it takes a conversation or two with a woman. They like to share their feelings."

"That they do, Jeremiah."

"That's why I've been married fifty years. I let my wife talk."

Colt didn't see how she had a chance to talk. He'd had conversations with Jeremiah. It usually included Colt listening to his neighbor, and Jeremiah talking for an hour without taking a visible breath. Maybe Jeremiah was making up for the times that his wife talked and he didn't?

"Well, Jeremiah, guess I should get to bed. I've got an early day tomorrow."

"Uh-huh." Jeremiah walked out on the porch. "Is that what you did to Lexi when the two of you were married, tell her you had to go to bed."

Colt looked away. Small towns were great, but

there was something to be said about the ano-nymity of living in a city where people couldn't use phrases like "Known you since you were knee-high to a grasshopper," and feel as if that gave them a right to get into a guy's personal business.

"Yep, that's a man thing to do." Jeremiah laughed, a deep chuckle in the still of an autumn night, reminding Colt that his neighbor was still on the porch. "Go on to bed, Colt, but you might want to work on that listening thing. That's what my wife always tells me. She says, 'Jeremiah, don't just listen, you need to actually hear what I'm saying.'"

"Thanks, Jeremiah. I'll keep that in mind."

"That's listening, not hearing." Jeremiah shook his head and walked back into his house, the door shutting softly behind him.

Colt stood in the yard for a few more minutes. He looked up at the stars, wondering about God and where He really was. People looked up, because that's where they imagined Him. But Michael had said something the other day: "God is as close as our heart if we will only let Him in."

God isn't up there somewhere, or out there in the distance. He's right here, all the time, waiting for us to call on Him.

Waiting.

Colt sat down on the porch step and Chico

pushed his head into Colt's arms. "Buddy, I've made a royal mess of my life and Lexi's. If God *was* right here, I think I've pushed Him away, too."

Pushed away, because a twelve-year-old Colt couldn't understand how his family watched half of their ranch being auctioned off to pay his dad's medical bills after a tractor accident and still went to church on Sundays to thank God for what they had left. God hadn't answered their prayers for the insurance company to pay for those surgeries.

God hadn't answered his prayers the night he found Gavin bleeding at the side of the road.

And now, how many prayers were being lifted up for a child named Kasey, for a lost dog, for a town that was trying to rebuild.

Colt bowed his head. Not really to pray, but to think, because he wondered, he often wondered. He knew God. He knew the reality of faith. He knew the ache of letting down the people he cared about.

And God, because the world wasn't a perfect place, didn't intervene when a police officer was shot down, or a tornado barreled toward a town, leaving behind miles of destruction. When those things happened, where was God?

A prayer away. The thought slipped into Colt's mind, almost a whisper.

"I want to have faith, God. I want to believe You

have answers. But how do I trust? How do I let go and let You take care of the people I care about?"

And what did he do with the feelings for his ex-wife, feelings that he had tried to convince himself were fading. He'd done a good job over the last two years, telling himself he was moving on. The only thing he'd managed to do was move his stuff to another house.

That wasn't really moving on.

# Chapter Six

On Thursday, Lexi had promised to help plant trees, replacing those that had been blown down on the town green along the river and next to some of the businesses. She pulled her truck into a parking space and saw Jill, along with a few others, already digging holes.

Lexi grabbed the pick and shovel she'd brought from home and walked toward the group. Jill waved and pointed toward the church. The blue Jeep that Colt drove.

"Any idea what he's doing at the church?" Jill didn't wait for Lexi to reach her, but tossed the question out from twenty feet away.

Lexi shook her head. "None of my business."

"You have to wonder." Jill pushed her shovel into the ground and, with her foot, pushed it a little farther. "Do you think they've found the ring? Or maybe Tommy's dog?"

"Not a clue, Jill."

"That's what we need. We need clues." Jill laughed, because she was being purposely annoying. Lexi ignored it.

"Where do you want me to dig?" She set her shovel and pick down and pulled on leather work gloves.

"About ten feet over." Jill nodded in the general direction. "He's been there for forty-five minutes."

Lexi picked up her shovel and moved away from her friend. She pushed it into the ground, scooping one shovelful of earth out of the ground and on the next attempt, hit a rock. She moved the shovel to a new spot and hit more rocks. "Wonderful."

"How is your house coming along?" Jill asked, leaning on her shovel. She had her hole nearly big enough for the tree.

"About like everything else in this town." Lexi glanced toward Main Street. Not the most heavily damaged area of town, but the most visible. Windows had been replaced and stores cleaned up. "What I wouldn't give to be able to walk into Hair and Nails for a pedicure."

That might not happen for a long time.

Businesses that she loved, people she cared about, and some would never return. Her heart ached at the thought. Life brought changes, she knew that, but letting go wasn't easy. At least she had faith. And since the tornado, her faith had grown. She had seen God work in so many little ways.

"The town does look better." Jill had returned to the hole she was digging. "When it first happened, I wondered if we would get to this point. Things are slowly returning to normal."

"I hope the churches don't."

"Do what?" Jill paused short of reaching for the tree she was about to plant.

Lexi dug at the hole with the pick she'd brought, trying to pry the rock loose so she could keep digging. It was hot, and perspiration trickled down her cheeks. "The good thing about this tornado was the way people came together. People turned to God and they didn't give up. Instead everyone seemed to get stronger."

"You have a point. Of course, there are the few people who wondered why God didn't stop it from happening."

Lexi glanced in the direction of the church, where the Jeep was still parked, and she nodded.

People like Colt. It was the police officer side of his nature, always investigating and seeking answers, thinking there has to be more to the story. Colt wanted to protect everyone.

She shrugged off the resentment that tried to

edge into her heart. She knew that Colt blamed God. What he failed to see was God's grace in the situation.

He failed to see the good that had come of this tornado and the lives that had been changed for the better. Every time she saw Greg Garrison and Maya, Lexi wanted to shout, it made her so happy. When she saw Heather next to Michael on Sunday mornings, what a wonderful blessing.

It helped Lexi to focus on those good stories that had come from the tragedy of the tornado. Even Jesse Logan was putting his life back together. Jesse and his three babies.

Lexi had a feeling these stories were only the beginning of the happy endings the tornado would provide for High Plains. She had been reading back over the history of the town, and she knew that the 1860 storm had brought similar, life-altering tales of love and bravery. Those stories were recorded as the history of the town. And someday this storm would be recorded in history, and the faith people turned to would be an example for others to follow.

"Lexi, are you going to beat that rock to death?" Jill laughed a little, but her tone was serious, maybe a little worried.

Lexi looked up, smiling when she glanced into the hole, at the crumbled remains of the rock that had gotten in her way.

"At least I can dig the hole now."

"We were talking about your house. When is it going to be finished?"

"He says four months. But he said that depends on everything he has to do. I don't know."

"Are you sure you can trust this guy."

"My parents gave me his name."

Jill's nose scrunched. "I know, I know."

"I want to get this done and get back to living my life, not feeling like everything is on hold." She smiled, getting it. "You think my parents sent someone who would sabotage the house and then I'd be forced to move back to Manhattan."

"The thought crossed my mind."

"Yeah, it crossed mine, too. But that wouldn't make me move back."

"What would?"

Lexi glanced in the direction of the church and the blue Jeep. "Nothing would make me move. But I have considered it, just because I know that eventually I have to let go, and I don't know if I can let go while I'm living here."

"Did Glenn call and ask you out?"

Lexi looked up. Now this was a conversation she didn't want to have, not now, when she was thinking so seriously about moving on and not letting Colt continue his happy dance in and out of her life.

"I think he left a message. Do you think he's the answer for my letting go?"

"He's a nice guy."

"Yes, he is. Maybe you should go out with him."

Jill laughed—really laughed. A few people turned to look at them. "I don't think so, honey. Blake asked me out last night. I'm pretty happy with that change of events."

The cowboy that Jill had loved forever. That sounded like a perfect happy ending.

"I'm happy for you."

A car started. Lexi glanced in the direction of the church. Colt was in the Jeep. Michael was standing next to it, talking through the open window.

"Please don't let him stop," she whispered for only God to hear.

Colt glanced in the direction of the town green and saw Lexi. Michael followed his gaze and chuckled a little.

"This is the time to start putting what we've talked about into practice, Colt."

Colt nodded, but he didn't want to go there. He had spent an hour talking. Talking about talking. And talking about listening. They also talked about him not being responsible for what happened to Gavin. It hadn't been easy, to call Michael Garrison and admit that maybe he needed to talk to someone. Counseling. He didn't really want to say the word. He could handle things. He could work through his own problems.

But then again, maybe he couldn't.

He obviously hadn't handled his marriage.

He shifted into Reverse, but Michael hadn't moved away from the side of the Jeep. Colt looked up, waiting.

"Colt, don't be so hard on yourself. We all make mistakes. We all look back and think we could have done something differently. You have a chance to maybe work things out, if that's what you want. So move forward and stop looking back—at things in the past that you can't change."

"I'm not sure what my next step should be. I think that moving too fast is a mistake."

"Fine, but whatever move you make, make a move toward having faith. Talk to your parents about the farm, and about their faith. See it from their perspective and maybe that'll help yours."

"Yeah, I'll talk to them. Gotta run."

"Okay." Michael stepped back and motioned for him to back out.

Colt planned to drive on past Lexi, but he didn't. She was shoveling dirt out of a hole, pretending she didn't see him. He smiled a little, because he knew that she had seen him at the church. He had watched her watching him.

She loved hard work. The first time he'd taken her home to meet his family, she had acted as if farming was the greatest treasure in the world. He knew that his family was the treasure she was seeking. She loved feeding cattle. She loved cooking big meals and sitting at the table together, not alone.

What had that been like as a kid, fixing her own meals, doing homework by herself at night? He pulled into the parking space next to her truck and killed the engine on the Jeep. She stopped shoveling and Jill said something to her, something that made them both laugh.

This was like being sixteen again. Or even twenty, in college and seeing her across campus, walking to her dorm. She wasn't that young woman anymore. She had proven in the last two years that she didn't need him. She could take care of herself.

He got out of the Jeep and walked to where the two of them stood—Jill and Lexi—swigging water from bottles and waiting. Jill put the cap back on her water bottle. He'd known her all his life and she'd never cut him any slack.

Today she did. "See you all later. I have a tree to plant by the creek." And she was gone.

"She didn't have to leave." He watched Jill go.

Lexi laughed. "You really didn't want her to stay. You know she'd give you a hard time. What are you up to?"

He didn't want to tell her that he had asked Michael to talk to him, to show him how to fix his life. Michael had told him the fixing part was between Colt and God. And Lexi, if he meant to fix his broken marriage. How did you fix something that was over? How did you dump a pie out of the pie pan and then stick it back in, whole?

He didn't think it worked that way.

"Have you discovered who the ring belongs to?" Lexi was asking. She had the tree and was trying to position it in the hole. He picked up the shovel.

"Hold the tree, and I'll shovel the dirt in around it," he offered, and she nodded. "No, I don't have a clue. Literally."

She smiled a little. "Maybe you should ask women who were recently engaged. I've sort of been thinking about this. Do you think someone might have taken the real ring because they found it somewhere after the storm, and then they realized whose it was, and they didn't want to give it back? Maybe they wanted to keep it because of its history. A ring like that has been on a lot of fingers and witnessed a lot of happy marriages."

She was still a romantic.

"You've sort of been thinking about this, huh?" He looked up and she was watching him. He couldn't look away, not from those dark blue eyes and that serious frown. She was beautiful when she was serious like that.

"I might have given it some consideration." She stepped down on the soil he had shoveled around the base of the tree. "It'll be beautiful when these bloom next spring. It's been sad, seeing so many trees without leaves, or the tops gone. I miss green."

"Next spring will be better." But he couldn't take his eyes off her, because her beauty distracted him, and he couldn't really think about trees. "So, how do I decide what woman—or man—would want a ring with history?"

"Talk to newly engaged women. Look at the past issues of the paper and see who announced an engagement."

She was beautiful *and* smart. Probably miles from the real truth about the ring, and this felt like a wild-goose chase, but he could check it out. It was better than anything he'd come up with.

"Colt, about the other night…"

He put a hand on hers and shook his head. "Lexi, I messed up. You've tried to take some of the blame, but this marriage ended because I wasn't there for you."

"You could try having faith. And maybe trusting that I'm stronger than you think. I know I wasn't strong at the time. But I am now." She didn't smile. She didn't turn away. She only stared, waiting for him to say the right thing.

And his phone buzzed as a call came in. He grimaced because he knew this wasn't the right way to start this conversation—the right track to take. "I have to get this."

"I know." She picked up her shovel. He thought she might walk away. She didn't.

He answered the call and when he dropped the phone into the pocket of his shirt, he felt a little hopeful. "Someone saw a guy walking down one of the farm roads and he had a dog with him. The dog looked like Charlie. I'm going to go check it out. The caller said he would meet me out there."

She nodded, because he should go. "Call and let me know what you find out. If it's Charlie, he might be injured or sick. Eight weeks is a long time."

The look in her eyes told him more. Eight weeks was enough to cause them to give up hope. But she had been praying. She was always praying. And he had seen her make it through so much and still smile, still have faith.

"What's Tommy going to do if we can't find that dog?" Colt knew the answer. The kid would be devastated.

"He'll survive, Colt. I know that you think this has been a tragedy, something completely unfair, but you have to look at the big picture."

"The big picture?" The kid had lost his dog. His best friend.

She gave him a sympathetic look, as if she knew what he was thinking. Of course she knew. She knew him. "Colt, he has a family now. If the tornado hadn't happened, if Greg Garrison hadn't hauled him inside that day, if Charlie hadn't disappeared…"

He raised his hand to stop her, because he got it.

"Tommy would have been in a new foster home by now. Uprooted once again."

His answer brought a smile, and she nodded.

"That's what I think. He'd still have his dog, but he wouldn't have Greg and Maya." Tears flooded her eyes. "And I still have hope that we'll find Charlie."

She was beautiful. And for that moment, the faith of a little boy danced inside his heart, and he wanted to believe, too. She did that for him. She created moments inside him that felt like Christmas morning.

Man, he really wanted to kiss her. He even took a step forward. And then he couldn't. She cleared her throat and gave him a look that asked what he thought he was doing. And he didn't have a clue.

But he did know that kissing her right now would be a mistake. He couldn't confuse everything with a connection like that. He didn't want to give people in town more reasons to talk about them.

He didn't want more to think about, to try and figure out. Not yet.

"I've got to go." He saluted and backed up a step before he turned and hurried to the Jeep.

"Call me later," she said, nodding. Her tone was still hesitant. He glanced back and waved. "Let me know about the dog. If it's Charlie."

"I'll call."

## Chapter Seven

Even though she'd worn gloves, Lexi's hands were blistered from digging holes to plant trees. She looked down at the raw spots and winced as the cold water from the sink hit them. Glancing out the window she could see the frame going up on what would be her new home.

She had the next couple of hours free. For now her plan was to go through what she had salvaged from the debris that had been her home two months earlier. She had a few boxes. The rest had been scattered around the countryside, or ruined by rain.

A cat inside one of the cages mewed. Lexi opened the latch and the calico walked out, a little timid, but sweet. Lexi picked her up and walked to the corner of the shop building, now designated as a bedroom. The cat curled up on the rug next to Lexi.

"Kitty, this isn't much to have left after thirty-one years." There were people with less. She closed her eyes and fought the wave of pain that sometimes swept over her. Michael had assured them all that it was normal to feel this loss, and to wonder if life would ever be normal again.

The people of High Plains were shell-shocked. They laughed, they smiled and they went on with life. But sometimes it hit them—the loss, and the weariness of rebuilding.

Lexi picked up a framed picture of herself and Colt a year after their wedding. It was the one picture she had left. Lexi had been twenty-three and she had believed this man would change her life. He was going to give her happy moments, and a family. They were going to build a life together.

And for six of the seven years, it had been a wonderful dream. They had finished college. Lexi had finished veterinary school. They had bought a home together and talked about having babies.

Lexi pulled the cat into her lap, but she couldn't stop looking at the picture. A young couple, smiling, ready to face the world and make their dreams come true.

Shortly before Gavin's death, they had decided it was time to start a family. They had jobs, a home and a future. After Gavin got shot, everything changed. Colt pulled away. Searching for the man who'd shot his fellow officer had consumed his every waking moment.

And he made a decision then to put off having children.

That had been the beginning of the end.

Lexi brushed at her eyes and put the picture away, wrapped in a pillowcase to protect the glass, but out of sight because she couldn't handle the reminder of what she'd lost. She couldn't go back, remembering the night he'd lain next to her, telling her that he couldn't think about having children when every day he went to work not knowing if he would come home.

He loved her too much to do that to her.

And he hadn't been willing to seek help, to talk to someone. She closed her eyes, remembering how she'd pleaded, telling him it was normal to feel as if a person's life was out of control after a tragedy happened. Stages of grief.

Instead he had retreated into a shell that closed her out.

And she had gone to church, finding real faith for the first time in her life. That faith had sustained her.

A car stopped out front. She didn't get up. The cat was on her lap and Lexi had pulled her jewelry box out of the pile of leftovers. She had jewelry that her parents had given her and jewelry from grandmothers. But her wedding ring was gone. It had been in a box in the closet, out of sight. It had bothered her to see it each time she reached in for jewelry to wear to special dinners or church.

A loud knock on her door jerked her from the memories. She blinked away tears, put the jewelry box down and stood. The pounding continued.

"Coming. I'm coming." She hurried to the front door, peeking out the window before unlocking it to let Colt inside.

"It isn't Charlie." He held a small tricolored sheltie in his arms. "But she might be about to have puppies. I mean, really ready."

"Let's have a look at her." Lexi lifted the sweet, pointy nose of the sheltie, and the dog whimpered. "You're a sweet girl."

"No collar."

"I hope she wasn't dumped." Lexi pointed to the examining table, and Colt lowered the dog. "She's thin. Maybe a tornado victim, but I haven't heard of anyone looking for a sheltie."

"I haven't, either." His words were clipped, terse.

"What's wrong?" She glanced up, still stroking the sable, collie-marked dog.

"I'm just tired. I've been getting a lot of middle-of-the-night calls. And then we have situations like this, with some guy trying to pawn a dog off as Charlie. For the reward."

"Do you think this dog is actually his?"

Colt shrugged. "Could be. She seemed to know him. But he asked me to find her a home."

"That really breaks my heart." Lexi stroked the long fur of the dog that looked like a miniature collie. "But we'll take good care of you, sweetheart. Maybe we'll even find her real owners. And she is going to have puppies. Soon."

"Wonderful." Colt shook his head. "What do I do with her?"

"What a silly question. You leave her here, of course. I don't have another kennel, but I'll fix her a place."

"Just what you need, another dog."

Lexi lifted the dog and carried her to a corner of the office. She glanced over her shoulder at Colt. "Get towels out of the cabinet. And don't be so mean. She deserves a home. Besides, I plan on adopting out most of these animals on Saturday."

"And keeping this one?"

"Of course." She sat on the floor next to the sheltie and smiled up at Colt. "I'm going to name her Lassie."

"Very original." He handed her the towels. "Now what?"

"We give her space and wait to see if she has her puppies. I don't think it'll be long." She stroked soft fur. "I'm going to get her some food and water."

"Can I help?"

"No, I'm fine." She rummaged through the cabinet and found a set of food bowls. "Do you want coffee?"

He didn't answer. She turned and saw that he was sifting through the boxes. "Is this all you have left?"

She nodded and filled the bowl with water. "That's it."

"I'm really sorry, Lex."

"You don't need to be." But her heart ached because she had lost her wedding pictures, and the photographs that chronicled the seven years they'd had together.

People had lost more. She realized that some of her neighbors had lost so much more.

She gave the dog food and water. Colt was looking at their anniversary picture. He glanced up when she walked toward him, holding it for her to see.

"They were a happy couple, weren't they?"

"They were." She took the picture away from him and stuck it back in the box. "But then, they weren't."

"Because he wasn't there for her." He met her gaze before looking away. "And when I was there, I didn't listen."

"We weren't very good at communicating." She

could smile now. "You should have been better. Your parents talked. Mine didn't. They left messages."

"I think you left me a few of those, too." Colt exhaled and shook his head. He looked out the window, at the skeleton frame that would be her home. "How's your house coming along?"

"Good, and you're changing the subject. You start to get close to talking to me, and then you go off in another direction, a direction that doesn't matter."

He shrugged, his back still to her. "I'm going to work on that."

"I'm glad." She moved next to him, and he turned—just a breath away—close enough to touch. "Two people who loved each other, who never stopped loving each other, shouldn't have given up so easily."

"You're right, they shouldn't have."

He brushed a hand through his hair and glanced back out the window, away from her, at the house she would live in alone. The house she wouldn't raise a family in. The house where she wouldn't wait at the door for him to come home at the end of a long day.

Because she didn't want to be jealous of his job, of a dead man, of a wife whose husband had died too soon. She didn't want to resent those people.

Lexi was shaking and it wasn't cold. Colt turned away from the window and he growled a little and pulled her close, wrapping her in arms so strong and safe that she felt as if nothing should hurt her ever again.

But it did hurt.

"I'm so sorry, baby, so sorry." He nuzzled her hair, kissing next to her ear and his arms didn't let go and finally she stopped shaking. "I'm trying to work through the mistakes I made. I'm not sure what the future holds, but I want you to know that I realize I made mistakes, and I wish I could take so much of it back. There are a lot of things I'd do differently."

Lexi stayed in his arms, snuggling against a solid chest that felt familiar, trying not to think about moving away and why she shouldn't let him hold her this way. "I think we both made mistakes and we'd both do things differently."

The first whimper of a puppy broke into the conversation. Lexi pulled out of his arms, feeling chilled and missing his touch. He brushed her hair back from her face and touched her cheek.

"I'm talking to Michael."

She shook her head, not getting it. "What?"

"I met with Michael today. I'm working on my life. On faith. I'm trying to let go of the past and find a way to stop being angry with God."

"Because of Gavin?"

"Us. Gavin. The farm."

"I know that bothered you, Colt. It was your family legacy. But your parents are happy. They still have the house and they have land. Most of all, you have your dad."

"I get that, Lex. I do get it, but that doesn't make it easier. It wasn't easy, watching them praying together. I stood there at the edge, wondering why God wasn't doing something to help."

"You were a kid. I'm not sure why, but I think you blamed yourself, or maybe you thought you could fix it?" She stood on tiptoe and kissed his cheek. "And then you blamed yourself for Gavin's death, and his wife left alone to raise their children."

"Kids without a dad."

Which is what he feared for her. "You could stop being a cop."

His mouth opened. "I…"

"I'm not serious." She reached for his hand. "I wanted to shock you and maybe make you think. There are safer jobs, but there are no guarantees in life. Look at what this tornado did to this community. It's about faith, Colt."

"You have puppies." He nodded past her.

"And you're changing the subject."

He grinned—a half smile that did things to her heart. He looked down at the ground and then met her gaze head-on. "Yeah, I am, but I think I've taken the listening thing as far as I can for one day.

I think you should take care of those puppies and we should go out to dinner."

"Out to dinner?" Lexi squatted next to the two puppies.

"Yes, out to dinner. You, me and maybe a little hope that we're on the right track. At least for healing and letting go."

"Is that the direction we're going?"

"I think it is. I hurt you and I don't want to have that be our story, as you put it in the basement that day."

She looked up, unsure, really unsure. "People in town will talk."

"We'll drive into Manhattan and go somewhere secluded, where no one will recognize us."

"What if we see my parents?" she teased, picking up one of the still-damp puppies.

"They'll be shocked?"

"They would be." Now was the time to tell him that she was considering moving back. And maybe working things out with Colt was good, because it would help her leave without leaving things undone.

He was looking at her and she couldn't tell him. Not yet.

"So, dinner?" He sat next to her.

"Sounds great." Or maybe it sounded like a big mistake that would hurt later.

The restaurant they picked was in an older part of Manhattan, on a quiet street, far removed from the hustle and bustle of the city. Lexi sat across from Colt, the candlelight glowing between them and silence. He didn't know what to say to her. It was like a first date.

And he was out with the most beautiful girl in the world. Her skin glowed and candlelight flickered. This restaurant had been one of their favorites, years ago.

The waitress approached with their dessert. "Would you like coffee?"

Lexi nodded. Colt shook his head and moved his water glass for her to refill it when she had time. As the waitress walked away, Lexi dipped her fork into the creamy cheesecake and took a bite. She closed her eyes, opening them when he laughed.

"Is it good?" He knew the answer. She loved cheesecake. Sometimes she made up the box kind and ate the filling from the mixing bowl.

"Very." Her expected answer.

Colt's phone buzzed. Lexi swallowed a bite of cheesecake and looked at him. She was waiting to see what he would do, and he knew he would fail the test. He couldn't ignore a call from one of his officers.

"I'm sorry, Lex."

"I know."

He flipped it open and smiled at her, hoping to ease the sudden wave of tension. As he answered, he kept his eyes on her, and she continued to eat the cheesecake. Instant replay, a scene that had played out a few too many times in their marriage. And sometimes it hadn't been an emergency. Toward the end, he had been looking for ways to escape.

He could see that now. He could see that, in a way, he had become her father, always busy. And he hadn't realized it then.

"That was Lucas, my new officer. He received a call in response to that article about Kasey. A family claims she's theirs, and they want to see her, immediately."

"Poor Nicki."

"We don't know if these people are her parents, Lexi." He reached, and she slid her hand into his. "But if they are…"

"I know. And I know that they might show up and claim their child. That's what should happen. But it won't be easy, to watch Nicki having to let go of that child. She's let go of a lot in life."

"She'll have the support of her friends."

Colt had to admit that seemed like a pretty poor substitute for a child the entire town, especially Nicki, had grown to love.

The drive to High Plains seemed to take forever. Colt drove fast, not too fast, his emergency lights flashing blue into the dark sky. Next to him, Lexi worried the tissue in her hand, not wiping eyes that were dry, but scrunching the poor defenseless thing into a wrinkled mess.

"Try to relax." He glanced her way again and she smiled.

"I really don't want this to happen. It's hard to know how to feel about this situation. You want a child reunited with her parents, but you don't want to see someone you know hurt."

"Where is God in this, Lexi?" He didn't mean to growl the words, but it happened and her gaze flew to him, her mouth opening a little.

She blinked a few times, but he could see that she was mentally gathering her thoughts. Of course she wouldn't let him get away with that.

"I can't answer that, Colt. I only know that I can look back and see how He has worked in so many things, and for that reason, I have to trust Him in this."

He nodded, because he really wanted to believe that God did have an answer, and that Kasey wouldn't be hurt.

They cruised through High Plains to the police station. A patrol car was parked out front and another car was parked in the lot to the side. The big doors of the fire station were open and the volunteer firemen were cleaning the fire truck.

Colt got out and, before he could open Lexi's door, she was out and waiting for him on the sidewalk. He started to reach for her hand but she shook her head. And he agreed, they weren't going there. This had to be about letting go and moving forward.

They walked through the doors of the police station, and the couple stood up. Colt didn't want to, but he had to admit the woman looked a little like the child that had been found after the tornado. He picked up a tablet on the desk. Head down, he perused the two people in shoes that were so new they had no scuff marks and clothes that didn't appear to have been worn before this night. They looked professional. They looked successful.

But where had they been for the last nine weeks? No one had reported losing a child, a daughter, a granddaughter. Kasey had been the child no one seemed to be missing.

Suspicions formed in Colt's mind. A quick look in Lexi's direction confirmed that she probably thought the same thing. The mother-bear look on her face worried him, though. She had the look of someone about to run some people out of town. He touched her arm, shooting her a warning look that she countered with a look of her own.

"I think I'll talk to you folks in my office." He motioned the couple down the hall. Lexi took a seat in the outer office. He needed an antacid.

"We want to see our daughter." The woman had tears in her eyes.

"Ma'am, we'll talk and if she is your child, we'll definitely get her to you."

"Her name is Maggie."

"Have a seat." He pushed the door to his office open and motioned the couple inside.

"We heard she was injured." The couple sat down, holding hands and waiting for him to answer. He sat down behind his desk in a chair that was normally comfortable. He leaned forward, watching the two people in front of him, wondering what their game was.

He had to admit, they looked worried about the child. They seemed to want answers. So why were the hairs on his neck bristling? He rubbed the back of his neck, trying to release the tension building in his muscles. He had taken this job after Gavin's death, thinking it would be less stressful than the job as a state trooper.

"She was banged up, but nothing serious."

"Is she okay now?" the prospective mother asked, wiping watery eyes with a tissue, crumpled like the one Lexi had held on to in his truck.

Lexi. He sighed and listened to the couple. How

did parents allow nearly two months to pass before they came to claim their child?

"I have to admit, I'm curious as to where you've been and how your child got here—in High Plains. Alone."

He sat back in his chair, arms crossed and doubts whirling through his mind as he watched the couple scramble for an answer.

"We were in Europe."

"For two months? Who had your daughter?"

"My sister had her. We don't know where my sister is. We haven't heard from her."

"Well, the funny thing is, we haven't had any missing people reported in this area. And no one has reported a missing child. We've been watching the national reports. No one matching this child has been reported missing."

"We hired an investigator." The man looked a little shocked, a little outraged.

"Could you tell me why you waited?"

"We were gone. I had business." The man again.

"We just want our daughter back." The woman leaned forward, biting her bottom lip, looking genuine. Colt nodded.

"Do you have her birth certificate? And we'll obviously need more proof. Family photographs, something with fingerprints, a DNA test. Oh, and there are medical bills."

"The media said that money has been raised to help pay for her medical expenses. Is there any of that money left?" The father shifted in the chair.

Colt sat forward again. Nicki Appleton loved a child that wasn't hers. Lexi wanted a family to love. And these people? He couldn't begin to think what they wanted. He realized it probably had a lot to do with money.

"The money has been spent to pay for her care and to buy what she needs."

"There's nothing left?" The woman looked up from the tissue, her gaze meeting Colt's. She didn't even look ashamed.

"The money is gone." It wasn't completely gone, but he liked the shocked look on their faces. The money that was left would go into an account for Kasey. "Can you describe her birthmark?"

The woman shook her head, "She doesn't have a birthmark."

"Sorry, *Mom,* you're out of luck." He stood, angry, tense, and the two people sitting in front of him had the good sense to stand up. "I think you should leave before I call the county prosecutor to see what charges we can file against you."

Colt sat back down, exhausted with this mess, with people that were so willing to take advantage of a tragedy. He buried his face in his hands as his blood pressure returned to normal. A light knock on the door interrupted thoughts that probably would·have shocked Reverend Michael Garrison.

He looked up. Lexi smiled, soft and sweet, like the first time he saw her. She didn't enter the room but waited at the door.

No longer his wife.

"Scam artists." He rubbed his hand over the top of his head before he leaned back in this chair. "Man, I hate this."

"But we love it for Nicki." Lexi, the optimist who wanted happy endings.

"Lexi, what about the parents of this girl? That's what I can't shake. There's a missing piece to this puzzle. There is someone missing, possibly in this town. And I don't have a clue. A parent could be dead. Or injured. Maybe kidnapped or harmed."

Lexi sat down across from him. "I know. I'm sorry. You see the case in front of you. I see a woman who desperately wants a child."

He saw that woman, too. She was sitting across from him. He looked at her and saw a child who had been neglected by workaholic parents. He saw a little girl dreaming of someday having a big family that went to church together and had big Sunday dinners.

She was talking about Nicole, not herself. He sighed and clasped his hands behind his neck, waiting for the tension to fade a little.

"What are you going to do?" Lexi asked.

"Keep looking for clues. Keep looking for her family. But two months, that's a long time. If she has family out there, even a grandparent, an aunt or uncle, why haven't they come forward?"

"I don't know." Lexi shrugged slim shoulders. "Colt, let's get out of here. You aren't going to find the answers tonight."

"I can't, Lex. I have to do some work."

She smiled a little smile and nodded. At the door she looked back, still smiling. "Colt, God isn't surprised by any of this. And you don't have to be alone."

And then she was gone, and she was wrong. He was alone.

## Chapter Eight

The yard around the High Plains Community Church was crowded with people, pets, tables of baked goods and some yard-sale items. Nearby, construction of the town hall had been suspended for a day. But it was coming along. They had the frame up and were about to start on the roof.

Today wasn't about building. Today was about fun, and coming together for one another. A band played a mixture of country and gospel music, and laughter carried from the dunking tank where Colt sat on the board, waiting to go under. At least it was still warm.

Lexi didn't want to hear him whine about being cold. The money raised was going to help those still in need within the community. And there were a lot of needs. People were still displaced and living in the Waters cottages that Heather had supplied after the tornado.

Families were still trying to replace what was lost, and not covered by insurance.

Lexi set the cages on tables that had been made with sawhorses and plywood. Kittens, puppies, even a goat and some chickens. As soon as the children saw animals, they came running.

She was the local petting zoo. And the animals really needed homes. Her feed bill for the last two months had been astronomical. Furthering the belief that her parents held: this was a bad career choice.

Two little girls with matching red pigtails and matching Kool-Aid smiles were the first to stop at the cage holding the sheltie and her new puppies. The puppies, four of them, were still curled against the momma dog's side, eyes closed.

"How are you girls today?" Lexi knelt next to Lilli Marstow and her friend Alyssa. The two eight-year-olds were constant companions. And a big source of contention between Josie Cane, who worked at the church day care, and Silas Marstow. The problems had started the day of the tornado, when the two girls had escaped together. Lilli's father, Silas, still grieving the loss of his wife, had blamed Alyssa's aunt, Josie.

Lexi thought the two adults should make up, for

the sake of the two girls. Lilli tugged on Lexi's hand. "How much for those puppies?"

"Honey, they're not for sale." Lexi's answer brought a frown to the sweet faces of both girls. The two actually looked like sisters. "I mean, they're free. But I can't give them away, yet. They'll need their mother for another six or seven weeks."

"Oh—" big frowns on angelic faces "—can we come back and see them, then?"

"Of course you can. But you have to ask permission. An adult needs to bring you."

"Okay." Alyssa was already sticking her fingers through the cage, petting a kitten. "I like kittens, too. I think Mr. Marstow is allergic."

"Okay." Lexi thought she might be missing something. But other children and parents approached and the girls scattered.

Tommy, still missing Charlie, peeked into the cage with the sheltie and her puppies. "Those are nice pups."

He sounded so big for his six years. She wanted to hug him and promise she'd find Charlie. Two months, though. She didn't see how it would happen.

"Tommy, do you want a corn dog?" Maya waved, but her smile was for Tommy. Greg Garrison came through the crowd behind Maya, her daughter skipping along next to him.

"No, I don't." Tommy shoved little hands into his pocket.

"I'm sorry, Tommy. You know, every time I go out on a call, I look for Charlie." Lexi smiled at the hopeful look on his little face. "But Tommy…"

He shook his head. "He's going to come back."

He ran off. Lexi watched him go, Maya close behind him, hugging him tight when he finally stopped. Lexi knew his little heart was breaking. She felt it as if it was her own pain. A hand, cold and wet, slipped into hers.

"It isn't easy." Colt gave her fingers a light squeeze.

"Children shouldn't have to hurt like that."

"No, they shouldn't. Maybe we will find Charlie, though."

She nodded and went back to her truck. She started to pull out posters and sheets for adopting animals, but first had to wipe her hands on her jeans. She looked back at Colt. His clothes were soaked.

"Your hands are wet," she teased.

"No kidding?" He pulled out his wet shirt. "What gives you that idea?"

"Things going well at the dunking tank?" She grabbed the posters and closed the truck door.

"The dunking tank is great. The water is cold, but that ensures that we earn more money. For some reason people love it when a cop is dropped into freezing cold water."

"I know, that's my favorite."

The sheltie, Lassie, whined a little, asking for attention. Lexi stopped at the cage and opened the door. She ran her fingers through the thick fur of the little dog and let the animal lick her fingers.

"What's this?" Colt pointed to the information hanging on the outside of the cage, information about the dog.

"I thought maybe her real owners would show up." Lexi closed the door after petting the little dog one last time.

"Lexi, you really like that dog, don't you?" Colt slipped an arm around her waist.

"She's sweet." The truth was, she let the dog have free rein of her temporary home. The puppies slept in a box. The sheltie slept with Lexi.

"Lexi, that dog's owner isn't going to come looking for her."

"What does that mean?"

Colt, handsome and always so sure of himself, turned a little red and looked away. Guilty. He was guilty and she didn't know why.

"What did you do?" She flipped his arm. He laughed a little, but she wasn't about to be amused.

"Okay, this is the thing. And you'll see, it's kind of funny."

"I'm listening."

"The guy that had the dog. It was his dog. He was willing to let me think she was Charlie because he wanted that reward. One problem, she's a girl. Oh, and the wrong kind of dog."

"You took the guy's dog?" She wasn't getting this.

"No, I didn't take someone's dog. I bought her from him. I knew you'd love her. He didn't want her."

Now she got it. She didn't know whether to punch him or kiss him. Quick, before she lost her nerve, she stood on tiptoe and kissed his cheek. And then she punched his arm.

"I'm not sure what to say to you." She looked away because her eyes were burning and she wasn't going to cry.

"Tell me you like your new dog?"

"She, I like."

"Me?"

She glanced up, not able to hide her smile. "You're okay, too."

A crowd had gathered and children were reaching in to pet animals. Kittens were mewing. The goat was out of her pen. A little boy tugged on Lexi's arm; in his other hand he had a kitten.

"I need to take care of some business." Colt stared at her for a long minute, making her think of days when he would have kissed her before walking away. "I'll be back, and you can lecture me then."

Lexi nodded and watched him go, tall and in control. And her heart was out of control, because it wanted to believe that she and Colt were working things out. More than that, she wanted the Colt that she'd known four years earlier, before they fell to pieces.

And she thought that the time they were spending together was his way of saying a final goodbye. It was time for that often spoke of *closure*.

Colt stopped when someone walked up behind him. He turned and wished he hadn't stopped. Michael Garrison laughed and shook his head. "That was cheesy."

"Excuse me?" Colt took a step away from his friend. "What was cheesy?"

"I'm not blaming you for trying to work your charm on her. But you passed the dog off as a stray?"

"I know, cheesy." Colt shrugged. "Actually, it's a little bit because of Chico. He was her dog and he wouldn't stay with her after the divorce."

"Try for real points. Come to church tomorrow."

"I might do that, but I'm not looking to earn points, Michael. Lexi and I needed this. We've skirted around each other for two years, avoiding being in the same room, the same place. We need to be able to be around each other without the tension." Colt held up the fake ring. "I need to talk to Missy Duncan." Newly engaged and possibly wanting a ring.

"Missy? Why?"

"I thought maybe she might know something about this ring."

"The ring that isn't the Logan ring. Why would Missy know about it?"

"I don't, Michael, I just like wild-goose chases. I thought maybe there might be a woman or man in this town that would have liked the Logan ring, because of what it stands for."

"That's not a Colt theory."

"No, it's a Lexi theory. They took the real ring, for the family history, and dumped the fake ring to get the heat off their back, allowing them a happy-ever-after with someone else's ring."

Michael laughed a little, with less humor. "Follow me. Have you talked to any other women in town?"

"Jamie Masters. Chuck proposed at the game. He was in the outfield and he held up a sign."

"Nice." Michael shook his head.

Colt thought *corny* was a better word. Lexi would have said it was romantic. Colt thought back to his own proposal. He had been more about tradition, because he knew that's what Lexi would want. She wanted it all. She had wanted the down-on-one-knee proposal, the traditional wedding, the house, the kids.

"How did you propose?" Colt asked his friend.

Michael shot him a look and shook his head, but Colt didn't miss the way his friend then glanced in the direction of Heather Waters. And he couldn't miss that maybe God had used this tornado to take care of unfinished business in a few lives.

Hard as it seemed, God was in control.

"There's Missy." Michael pointed. "I need to help Lexi match animals to people. You go match a ring to a con man."

"I didn't say she's the one." Colt shook his head. This wasn't working out the way he planned. "Michael, do you have any other ideas? Jesse wants his ring. This ring was tossed into your lost-and-found box. I'm the one who has to find answers—for this and a dozen other problems since the tornado."

Michael's brows shot up. "Colt, I'm not sure what to say about this. Other than you're taking it all on yourself. You have other officers. You have a community that supports you. You have a wife…."

"Ex-wife."

"Wife. You know you still love her. She still loves you."

"It takes more than love."

"It takes trust." Michael patted his back. "It

takes a willingness to talk and work through things. It takes the knowledge that there are no perfect relationships. And Lexi didn't ask you to carry it all for her."

"No, she didn't." Colt slid the ring onto his little finger and waved his hand. "I need to take care of this." He started to walk away, but he turned. Michael was still standing there. "Michael, I appreciate you. You're being honest. And you're probably right."

Michael laughed at that. "Of course I'm right."

Missy looked at him as if he was crazy when he asked to see her engagement ring. He felt a little crazy. He was actually following Lexi's advice on how to investigate a case. And he knew better.

When they were married she sent him on more wild-goose chases. Once she had called to tell him that someone was stealing laundry off an elderly neighbor's clothesline. It turned out to be a neighbor's dog, and the owner of the dog, embarrassed by the situation, was throwing the clothes in a bag and hiding them.

He glanced in Lexi's direction. She stood off to the side holding a kitten out to a little girl. When Lexi leaned, her hair fell forward. She pushed it back with her left hand. A hand without a ring. He looked down at the ring in his hand, the tiny diamond sparkling. He remembered putting the band on her finger the day they pledged to love one another forever.

He didn't remember seeing it in the box of things she'd salvaged after the tornado.

"Chief Ridgeway, do you have something you want to ask me?" Missy stared up at him.

"Missy, how did Frank propose?"

"What? I'm confused, what does that have to do with this ring?"

Not a thing. He sighed, and for the first time in his career he felt a little scattered. "It doesn't have anything to do with the ring, Missy. I'm not sure where this ring came from, or who put it in the lost and found. I'm trying to figure this out."

"And you think knowing how Frank proposed will help?" Her mouth twisted and she shook her head. "Okay, fine."

He pulled out his notebook, as if he meant it. Pen poised, he waited for her to talk. Her gaze flew past him. He turned and saw Lexi tying a rope to a collar on a goat. Missy chuckled a little.

"Interesting," she whispered.

"Interesting?"

"Frank proposed by putting an advertisement in the paper. It was the sweetest thing. Front page of the *County Herald,* he asked me to marry him."

"You're kidding." Colt thought he might be a little sick.

"No, I'm serious. Isn't that wonderful and romantic?"

"Romantic."

"Did you hear what Clark Gibson did?"

He couldn't wait. "No, I didn't."

"He bought a wedding ring quilt from the craft fair this summer. He had the ladies in the quilting group sew the engagement ring to the center of the quilt and had his name and Cathy's embroidered on it."

"Sweet." And a little nauseating. He wanted to ask another question. Would these couples make it? Would they stick to it, through the rough times, through doubts and pain?

He couldn't ask Missy that question. He could see that she believed in forever. And Lexi believed in it, too.

"Chief Ridgeway, it isn't any of my business, but I think you should just ask her to marry you again. You don't have to buy a quilt or take out an ad in the paper, just ask."

His mouth dropped and he shook his head, amazed that she had the nerve to make that statement. But hadn't he just questioned her about her proposal? Fair turnabout.

"Thanks for answering my questions." He shoved the ring back into his pocket and walked away.

Jesse didn't have his family heirloom. Couples

were falling in love, thinking of forever together, and other people were trying to figure out how to believe again, to have faith.

He fell into that latter category. He was trying to have faith, but people were willing to take a little girl for money they thought was available, and another man was willing to sell his own dog.

Sometimes people made it hard to have faith. But looking around—at the town green full of people who had gathered to help their neighbors—maybe faith wasn't so far out there after all.

The town was being rebuilt, but so were lives. He had only to look at Maya and Greg with their growing family, or Michael and Heather, to know how true that was.

"Chief!"

Colt turned, waiting for Junior to catch up with him. The older officer was out of breath, perspiration beading across his forehead. Junior was a county deputy, but assigned to the High Plains rural area.

"Hey, Junior."

"Chief, big news. Remember that Parsons guy?"

Colt nodded, but cold encased his heart. "Yes."

A man that had gone on a crime spree last year. It had taken several counties to run him down and finally catch him.

"He escaped."

*Escaped.* A man who had threatened to get Colt back, because Colt had been relentless in hunting him down.

Lexi. Colt caught her gaze and smiled. She waved.

"State wanted you to know," Junior continued. "He might head in this direction. He had a friend outside of town here."

"I remember." The friend had disappeared months ago. The house was sitting empty. No one wanted it. "Thanks, Junior. We'll be looking for him."

"Remember, I'm a radio call away if you need help."

"That's good to know." Colt worked hard at smiling. If Parsons was on the loose, they would need help catching him.

He walked away from Junior, thanking him for the information.

Now he had to add Lexi in danger to his list of responsibilities. And how could he protect her? He could no longer sit in the living room while she slept, waiting for danger to walk through the door.

He could pray. Lexi and Michael would both tell him that. He could trust that God had this in control. Lexi's favorite saying echoed in his mind: "God isn't surprised by this."

* * *

Lexi watched the last kitten being carried away by a little girl that promised to love the tabby—forever. When she looked up from the paperwork, she saw Colt heading across the lawn. He had been talking to a county officer earlier, and then he'd headed back to the dunk tank.

She smiled as he drew closer. "Hey, stranger, you're soaked again."

He stood in front of her, sopping wet. His sun-streaked blond hair was plastered to his head and water dripped down his face. Boyish and adorable. He had always been those things.

"We made a lot of money for the tornado relief fund."

"That's great." She grabbed an empty cage and shoved it into the back of her truck. "I would have paid a lot of money to see you go into that water."

"It was freezing cold."

"I'm sure it was. You should probably get into dry clothes and drink some tea to warm up."

"I have dry clothes in my Jeep. No tea, though."

Lexi bit down on her bottom lip and nodded. She reached for another cage. He got to it first. Their arms brushed. His was damp and cold.

"I can do this." She tried to take it from him.

"I'll help."

"Colt…"

He turned, his smile soft and the look in his eyes tender. He winked. Resolve melted away, like wax in a hot flame. "Lex, let me help you."

"This is too much."

"What do you mean?"

"I mean, I don't know where this is going, or how to process what is happening."

"I think this is me, trying to help you."

"Okay, you help me, and I'll make hot tea so you won't catch cold."

"Sounds like a great idea."

No, it sounded like a mistake and she couldn't stop herself.

## Chapter Nine

Colt took the cup of tea Lexi held out to him. Steam rose from the amber liquid, and the fragrance of herbs and jasmine was strong.

Lexi's hair fell forward. She brushed it back with her right hand, and the only ring she wore—her grandmother's engagement ring—caught his attention. She looked up, her gaze meeting his, and then she looked away.

"Lex, I noticed your wedding ring set wasn't in the box you had out the other day." He shouldn't have brought it up, but he couldn't let it go.

She shrugged slim shoulders as she walked back into her small kitchen. She opened a cabinet and pulled out a box of cookies. And she didn't answer, not right away. Colt moved to the edge of the sofa but he didn't get up. He wouldn't push her to go where she didn't want to go.

When she turned, her eyes were clear. Had he expected tears?

"They're gone. They were in a box in the hall closet."

"I'm sorry."

Another lift of her shoulders, as if it didn't matter. But it did. To him, it mattered. It probably shouldn't. Their marriage had ended two years ago. The rings were a symbol of something that had become broken and unfixable.

Even as he let those thoughts run through his mind, he wondered, was it unbroken, or had they just given up? He put the cup of tea down on the coffee table and walked across the room to stand next to her.

"Remember when we picked those rings out?" He bumped his shoulder to hers, wanting to make her smile.

"Yes, you told the jeweler that price was no object, and then you saw the price of the rings they brought out. I thought you were going to choke."

"You let me think you wanted the biggest one."

"It was fun, to see you look a little pale, maybe a little green."

Her hair fell forward, exposing a sweet spot next to her ear. He had kissed that place so many times. Even the day he bought the rings, as she looked over the half dozen that fit his budget.

He closed his eyes and remembered. And then he kissed her again, in her kitchen on a fall day with her rings missing and their marriage over. And it still moved him.

He kissed her neck and then her lips, tasting herbal tea and watermelon lip gloss. She kissed him back, her hands behind her back and her face tilted up.

Somewhere at the back of his mind he remembered that this was about letting go and moving on, not getting stuck in the past. But the past hadn't been bad. Their marriage had never been bad.

It had just been broken, by her fear and his.

He tasted the salt of her tears on her cheeks and then she moved away from him. He should have moved away first.

"I'm sorry," he whispered into her hair.

"I could have stopped you, so don't apologize."

"Okay, I won't. But that isn't why I came over here."

She nodded and turned away, and he could see where her tears had washed away her makeup. He had really messed up.

His radio squawked. He moved away from her and took the call. Parsons had been spotted outside of High Plains.

"Lex, I have to go."

"What's up?" Casual tone, as if she wasn't

worried. He remembered the tense voice in the last weeks of their marriage. And he remembered the night he had twenty missed calls on his phone, because she hadn't been able to reach him.

He wasn't going to lie to her. "Mitch Parsons escaped."

"Oh." She washed his cup, over and over. "I guess you do have to go."

"I do." He moved behind her. "You'll be okay?"

"Of course." She smiled at him, really smiled. "Colt, two years is a long time. I've learned to pray. I can admit that I still worry about you. But I'm not living in fear, always wondering when something bad will happen."

"Good." He stood at the door. "Lock your doors, though. Okay?"

"I'll lock them. I'm not going anywhere, anyway. I think something I ate made me sick."

"You're okay?"

"Of course. Go, Colt. I know you need to leave."

"I really am sorry. But I'm also glad we're talking. I think that both of us have been living in some kind of holding pattern for the last two years, not really moving forward."

"I haven't been waiting for you to come back."

"I know." But maybe he'd hoped, a little, that she wanted him back. "Oh, my mom wanted me to invite you out for Dad's birthday party at the first of October. She also said lunch after church tomorrow."

A party she hadn't attended for two years. He waited, his hand on the doorknob, and she was looking out the window. For the last two years she hadn't accepted invitations to attend family functions at the farm. He knew she missed them.

Working things out with her meant that she might let herself back into his family circle. She nodded, not looking in his direction.

"Tell your mom I'd love to go. I'll bring my broccoli salad."

"I'll let her know."

He walked out the door and a few steps away he heard the bolt click as she locked it. As he got into his Jeep, he saw her at the window, watching.

Lexi woke up Sunday morning as the sun was lighting the eastern horizon a faint pink and birds were beginning to sing in the new day. And she felt horrible. But she couldn't be sick. She was going to the Ridgeway farm for lunch. She'd had lunch with Colt's mom a month ago, but going to the farm— it felt special, like Christmas.

She sat up, ignoring the wave of nausea that rolled through her stomach. A cup of coffee would cure everything. She stood up, stretching to relieve the kinks from sleeping on the sofa and then she walked into the kitchen area. The sheltie's tail thumped on the floor. Lexi filled the dog's food and water bowls.

That reminded Lexi, she needed to call Josie about the puppies. She would let the girls work out a way to get their respective parents together, but Lexi didn't mind greasing the wheels a little by telling Josie the puppies would soon be ready if she wanted to bring her niece over.

Lexi smiled at the tiny puppies, maybe part Border collie, and still very cute. They would be easy to get rid of. And she needed to get rid of the nausea that had hit her yesterday afternoon. She filled a cup with water and sprinkled in ginger powder. She took a sip and closed her eyes. A cool breeze wafted through the open window. So did a funny noise.

*Beep, beep, beep*—the faint sound caught her attention. She peeked out the window and smiled. Colt with a metal detector. She knew what he was doing. He wanted to find her wedding ring. She watched as he made steady progress, step by step across the yard, around the frame of her new home.

Her heart got stuck in some strange place between aggravation and tenderness. She watched for a minute and then she turned to the fridge and pulled out a carton of eggs. He would need breakfast. It gave her something to do, a way to think through what she felt, rather than reacting.

It wasn't the ring. It was what it symbolized. They had lost so much, and the ring was one thing he thought he could give back. But what would it mean? She cracked eggs into a bowl and thought about having it back.

And she tried not to think about eggs. Maybe she had some donuts left?

She glanced back out the window, saw him digging in the dirt. And then tossing aside whatever he'd found. He still didn't know she was watching.

Her heart beat a little harder and she blinked the sting from her eyes. Of all the things lost in the tornado, those rings seemed low on the list of priorities. Her marriage was already over and the rings weren't going to fix anything.

But losing the rings had hurt more than anything else—the rings and her wedding pictures. She'd already lost Colt. Her marriage was over. The rings were more leftovers. Maybe she should have gotten rid of them sooner?

She heated butter in a skillet and poured the eggs in with a handful of chopped ham and shredded cheese. The beeping continued. The yard was full of metal.

"Hey, do you want breakfast?" She spoke through the open window. "Omelets?"

He turned; even from the distance she could see his smile.

"You don't have to."

"I don't mind."

He shrugged and headed for the house and memories flickered through her mind, him coming in for breakfast, the aroma of coffee and toast. She flipped the eggs and pretended it meant nothing.

Colt walked through the door, and her heart managed to convince her it meant everything. He shrugged out of his jacket and tossed it on a chair.

The room took on the scent of the outdoors and his cologne.

"No luck." He poured himself a cup of coffee and refilled her cup.

This was too easy. It felt like the easy rhythm of their marriage, as if they were picking up where they left off. But Lexi couldn't let it be that easy, not when her heart had been broken just a few years earlier.

The only thing missing was the hug. He had always walked up behind her, hugging her from behind as she cooked. And she had wanted children to fill their home. She had wanted a little toddler, sitting on her kitchen floor with bowls and wooden spoons to play with. She had wanted a little boy with blond hair, driving toy trucks through the dirt and coming in with smudges on a face with dimples.

She bit down on her lip as she slid the eggs onto a plate. Colt buttered the toast and set a second plate on the counter. No conversation to fill the silence. Lexi needed conversation.

"Are you still going to church this morning?"

"I am. After all, everyone else in town is going."

"Don't be sarcastic." She turned and he had the good sense to look guilty.

"You're right. I'm going because I want to. I've spent quite a few years ignoring things that bother me. Instead of confronting what happened with my dad, I got mad at God. I got a little mad at my family for still having faith. And when Gavin died, it fueled that anger. I'm working through it."

"I'm glad to hear that." And she didn't want to think about what it meant to her, or the marriage that was behind him. His anger had led to their divorce. So what happened when he was no longer angry?

Was that the reason for him being here now?

She couldn't ask. She didn't want to hear the answers. He might say yes. But if he said no, that would make it hurt all over again.

"Do you want to eat outside?" Easier than dealing with his faith, their marriage.

"Sounds good."

She picked up her plate and walked out the front door, to the picnic table she'd bought last week at the thrift store.

"Won't be too many more days like this, warm enough to eat breakfast outside." Colt sat down next to her. He looked a little scruffy, with something way past a five-o'clock shadow and the same clothes he'd had on yesterday.

"Colt, you slept in your truck last night, didn't you?"

He shrugged and took another bite of eggs.

"You don't have to do that." She pushed her plate to the side, because the smell was undoing what the ginger had done for her.

"I'm not going to apologize for caring about you." He nodded at her plate. "Why aren't you eating?"

"I feel terrible. I mean, not so bad I can't go to church, just not up to eating. Have you learned anything more about the ring? I've had another thought on that. Maybe someone put it in there thinking Jesse would be fooled and it would make him feel better. He's lost so much. Maybe they were trying to help?"

"There are a lot of 'could be's.' And let me tell you, these newly engaged couples…" He shuddered.

Lexi laughed. "A little too much romance for your old age?"

"If it's contagious, we're in trouble."

"I don't think we'll catch it." She sighed. "I'm sorry."

"You don't have to apologize. I think we've been doing too much of that. And to be honest, I like this, having you as a friend again. I don't want to mess that up."

"No, neither do I. But I also don't want either of us to get the wrong ideas."

"Can I ask you a question that Michael asked me to think about?" He turned to straddle the bench of the picnic table. "Can you be happy with someone else?"

Not a fair question. She had dated. She had endured blind dates, only to come home and wonder why she could still feel the presence of a man she was no longer married to.

"I don't know." She turned to face him, pulling one leg up to rest on the bench. "I can't imagine someone else in my life. In my heart you're still…"

*My husband.* She shook her head and stood up. "I have to get ready for church."

"You didn't eat."

"I really don't feel like eating."

Colt stood and picked up their plates. "Let me drive you. I'll pick you up in an hour?"

He was letting it go that easily? Or maybe they both had their answer. She nodded and took the plates from his hands, and hers shook. "In an hour."

When she closed the door, she could see him still in her yard, still looking puzzled. And she had a real estate brochure for Manhattan, Kansas, that he didn't know about.

Her mom was trying to convince her that moving on meant…moving. And maybe there was something to that. Moving away from the memories might make it easier to go on without Colt.

Lexi sat on the pew next to Colt, her hands in her lap and her head slightly bowed. He tried to listen to Michael, but couldn't pay attention because she was so still, so pale.

As the congregation sang, he reached for her hand. It was warm.

"'Pass me not, O gentle Savior, hear my humble cry, while on others thou art calling, do not pass me by…'"

Lexi's sweet voice sang the Fanny Crosby song, and he knew that she meant it. He knew her faith, that it was as much a part of her being as the oxygen she breathed. He knew that as a child she had wanted that faith, but hadn't understood. She had gone to church, thinking that by attending her home would be a happier place.

He sometimes wondered if she had married him because she wanted that perfect life, and she thought he was the key. He was a farm boy with a big family that shared Sunday dinners.

The congregation moved on to another song.

He tried to sing along, but his attention focused on the people and their faith. So many of them were still without homes. They were rebuilding their businesses. They were rebuilding their lives.

And they had faith.

The very thing he had pushed out of his life was sustaining these people and helping them to get through. Lexi stopped singing.

Her eyes closed and she leaned against him. "Could you take me home?"

The whispered words were a surprise. "Lex?"

"I'm really sick."

He glanced around. People were singing. No one seemed to notice. "Okay, let's get out of here."

He took her by the hand and slid out of the pew. She followed. A few curious glances. He smiled and nodded at a few people, but Lexi was leaning against him.

They got out the front door, and she rushed to the side of the building. He didn't follow. When she returned, her face was pale and her eyes luminous, shimmering with moisture.

"Come on." He wrapped an arm around her waist and led her to the Jeep. "Why didn't you tell me you were this sick?"

"I didn't realize. It was nausea earlier, but now it's worse."

"When did it start?"

"Yesterday. I think I have food poisoning. I had a chicken sandwich the other day." She groaned. "I don't want to talk about it. I might never eat another chicken sandwich."

He laughed a little as he helped her into the car. She shot him a look and then she leaned. He jumped back, cringing. So much for a perfect Sunday together.

"Are you going to make it home?"

He'd seen her like this before, but he didn't have a strong stomach. His compassion was strong, his fortitude when it came to a stomach ailment, not as much.

"You're just worried about your car," she teased in a weak voice as she clicked her seat belt.

"It was on my mind." He grabbed a box of tissues out of his console. "There are some antacids in there, too."

She shook her head. "Home, and a cup of hot peppermint tea."

"Gotcha."

When he got behind the wheel, she was shivering. Her eyes were closed.

"Lexi, should I take you to the hospital?"

She shook her head. "I'm fine. Last time I went to the hospital, you weren't there." Her eyes opened. "I'm sorry, that wasn't fair."

"It was fair."

"I keep remembering you looking in the back of the ambulance. And I didn't really see you again for a week."

"I had to…"

She lifted her hand. "I know. People needed you."

"Yes, people needed me." And he was an idiot. "And you needed me. I'm really sorry. I always see you as so strong, so independent."

A tear trickled down her cheek and she bit down on her lip, nodding just a little as she brushed the tissue across her face.

"I'm sick. Ignore me."

"We're almost home." Her home, not his. He eased down the street and pulled into her drive. The contractor was working on her house. Electricity had been run from the main line, giving them power on the job site.

"Thank you for bringing me home." She reached for her purse. He grabbed it first and handed it to her.

"Lexi, I'm not going to drop you off and leave."

"I'll be fine."

"I know you will." He pulled the keys from the ignition. "But I'm staying."

"I'm going to be sick," she whispered as he parked. And then she flung the door open and ran for the house.

"I think I might be sick, too." He shook his head and watched her run into the house.

He followed her inside and his conscience chided him. He had put her in that ambulance with nothing more than a goodbye. After six hours in the basement together, he had sent her off alone.

For the last two months he had ignored the obvious, that he wasn't good at being there for the people who needed him. She had asked him to go with her, and he had meant to, but when they finally got out of the basement, he realized the extent of the damage, and he had made the decision to stay in town and take care of search and rescue, as well as assessment of the damage.

So many people had needed him.

She had needed him.

Colt waited outside the bathroom for Lexi. This time, he wasn't leaving her alone.

# Chapter Ten

Lexi opened her eyes and blinked a few times, trying to get her bearings. She was comfortable and safe. She was curled up on the couch, her head against Colt's shoulder. A rerun was on TV and the puppies whined from their cage. But at her feet, Chico and Lassie. She blinked a few times and stretched, trying to remember what day it was, and if it was morning or night.

"How are you?" Colt's deep voice vibrated against her back.

"I feel great. Please don't mention chicken."

"Not even soup?"

She groaned and shook her head, but that made her head ache. Lexi closed her eyes and leaned into his chest, his arm holding her close. He felt so good. She had forgotten how everything felt right in the world when he held her like this.

"No soup," she whispered. "You should go. You're supposed to have lunch with your mom today."

"I called her. She said to stay with you. She also said you need to drink water—" he kissed her brow "—and you need more medicine."

"I'm good. You really don't have to stay." But she wanted him to stay. She couldn't tell him that. She hadn't been able to say it the day he'd packed his bags. Instead she had stood at the door, feeling as if her whole world was caving in around her.

She wouldn't beg anyone to stay and love her.

He got up and walked into the kitchen. She closed her eyes, but could hear him shaking pills out of a bottle and running water into a glass.

"I'm not going anywhere, yet." His voice sounded loud in the quiet room. "And when I leave, Jill is coming over. She can spend the night on your couch without starting a rumor."

A hand touched her head. "Here you go."

She opened her eyes, and he put the pills into her hand and then gave her the glass. She smiled up at him. "Thank you. You make a good nurse."

"If being a cop doesn't work out for me, I'll keep that in mind." He sat down next to her and she closed her eyes, glad that he was there. Later she could remind herself that it was a mistake.

It was a mistake because Colt couldn't change. She didn't want to come second behind a job.

When she woke up again, he was gone. She sat up, cold because he wasn't there. He was at the sink, filling a glass with water. Chico sat next to him, waiting for a treat. Lassie was curled in the curve of Lexi's knees, warm and cuddly, her pointy nose on Lexi's legs.

"When did they see him, Junior?"

Lexi held her breath, because she hadn't realized Colt was on the phone. He turned a little and she saw the earpiece.

"Is there anyone with him?"

She waited, knowing this was the telling time. She closed her eyes, wishing she didn't have to hear what she knew was coming.

"I'm fifteen minutes from there." Long pause. "I'll be there if you need me, but if you have plenty of officers, I'm staying here with Lexi. If things don't change, I'm taking her into Manhattan to the hospital." Another pause. "If you need to, you can call one of my city officers."

He ended the conversation and turned. When he saw her, he smiled a little, and she smiled back. "If you need to leave…"

"I'm not going anywhere, Lex." He sat down on the ottoman in front of her sofa and held out a glass of water. "Drink this."

She drank the water and then leaned back on the pillow he must have put under her head while she was sleeping.

"Colt, I don't want to do this to you. I don't want you to feel I'm keeping you from your job. I don't want you to resent me."

"I don't resent you." He took the glass from her hand. "Try to rest."

"While you pace and look out the windows."

"Don't take everything from me." He winked and she nodded.

Keeping people safe was a part of who he was. She knew that, had always known. "Colt, I don't want to change who you are."

Brows shot up and she had to explain. "Who you are is this wonderful man who cares deeply about people, and about keeping them safe. Sometimes, though…"

"Sometimes it becomes an obsession?"

She nodded again, but her head swam and she closed her eyes. His hand rested on her cheek, his fingers brushing lightly.

She couldn't forget that he had made a choice to stay with her. He moved to the chair and put his feet up on the ottoman.

The next time she woke up, Jill was in the chair that Colt had been sleeping in.

"Where did he go?"

"He's outside, Lex."

Lexi sat up, brushing a hand that trembled through hair that was tangled and needed to be washed. She reached for water and Jill pushed it close enough for her to reach. "What time is it?"

"Two in the morning."

"I feel like I might have eaten dirt."

"Chicken will do that to you."

Lexi groaned. "I think I'm dying."

Jill laughed and put her book down. "Nope. Colt called Doc and Doc said to bring you in tomorrow and he'll take a look and prescribe something."

"I've got antibiotics in the fridge." Lexi closed her eyes because the light was bright and her head was pounding as if little men were in her brain with hammers, trying to get out.

Jill laughed. "You want to give yourself a shot of something you give to Billy Faire's Holsteins?"

"Beats this."

"Go back to sleep."

Lexi shook her head and sat back up. She had to check on Colt. What if Parsons was after him? She must be getting better, because that thought hadn't crossed her mind until now. What if Colt was in danger?

"Where are you going?"

"To check on Colt."

"He's a big boy."

"Parsons is out there somewhere."

"And you don't want him to touch your man?"

"Don't be ridiculous. Colt and I have decided we can still be friends." But her legs shook and her stomach protested the movement. Lexi leaned against the counter and waited for the world to stop spinning. "This stinks."

"Frankie May has it, too."

"Food poisoning?"

"Yep. It was something at the carnival."

"I thought it might have been. I hope that more people don't get sick."

"Lexi, sit back down. I'll go out and check on him."

Lexi shook her head. "I don't want him to know we're checking on him. I just want to see for myself that he's okay."

"And that he's really out there?" Jill got up and followed Lexi to the window.

"I'm not checking up on him." Lexi stood to the side and peeked out the window, Jill close behind her. And there was his Jeep. The security light on the corner gave off enough light for her to see him inside.

He hadn't left.

As if he knew she was watching, he turned and waved. Lexi raised her hand to wave, and then she blew him a kiss. Because he hadn't left her.

* * *

Pounding woke Colt. He rubbed his face and then the back of his neck. Blinking against the early-morning light, he realized he was parked in front of Lexi's house and the pounding noise was the construction crew working on what was supposed to be her new home. He had slept in front of her house. He groaned and rubbed his face again.

Someone knocked on the window. He jumped a little and moved his hand off his face. Jill. She smiled and held up a mug of coffee.

Colt turned the key and rolled down the window. "Thanks for that," he mumbled.

"Scare ya?"

"Not at all. I'm always on the alert."

"Okay, we'll all believe that. Here's coffee. You should go home now."

Home. He glanced at the building being constructed next to Lexi's clinic and then at the clinic.

"Do you know she has real estate brochures for Manhattan?"

"What?"

Jill leaned against the side of the vehicle. "She had information from different Realtors in Manhattan, for homes and office buildings. I feel like a snitch, but I thought you should know."

"I didn't know." He leaned back, closing his eyes.

"Don't let her leave. Not if you still love her."

"Jill, I'm not going to get into this with you. Lexi and I are doing the best we can." He opened his eyes when Jill made a noise somewhere between a grunt and a growl. "What?"

"So, you're willing to let her leave?"

"It's too early for this conversation."

"That's a 'man' response. You don't want to talk about it. You messed up, my friend. You really messed up."

"Thanks for that. I need to go."

She rested a hand on his arm. "I'm sorry, I didn't mean to give you a hard time. Or maybe I did. But I wanted you to know that you're really close to losing her for good."

"Message received. Call if she needs me."

"Will do."

He drove down Main Street, remembering back to July. Clouds on the western horizon reminded him of how the air had felt that day, and how the wind had roared. Today the clouds were fluffy and white. The sky was robin's-egg blue.

But the General Store was still closed and the Old Town Hall was a pile of debris that they planned on burning soon. He looked out across the town green, at trees in the distance still wearing ribbons of sheet metal from barns that had been destroyed.

He wondered if it would ever be the same.

Of course it wouldn't. Nothing would ever be the same. As the town was being rebuilt, so were the lives of the people in High Plains. And some people had new lives.

As he drove, Josie Cane parked in front of the day care. He knew her schedule. She had probably dropped her niece, Alyssa, off at school and now she was going to work. He had seen Alyssa and Lilli Marstow, Silas Marstow's daughter, sneaking off to play on Sunday morning before church. He smiled, because he hadn't told on either of them. He had heard all about the two girls escaping after the tornado. It was wrong of them to do it. Just as wrong for Silas to try and separate them.

And, in Colt's opinion, the widower should give Josie a break. Actually, the guy ought to give himself a break.

Not that Colt could really give anyone advice on moving on.

His phone rang as he pulled up to the office. He didn't recognize the number. "This is Chief Ridgeway."

"Yes, sir. My name is Brent Carlson. I live about twenty miles north of High Plains."

"Yes, sir. How can I help you?"

"Well, this sounds a little odd, but I have something I think belongs to you. After the tornado, we found some wedding pictures in our field. We didn't have a clue who they might belong to, and then, the other day, we saw you on the news and realized that you're the guy in the pictures. We thought you and your wife might like to have these pictures back."

"My wife…" The words stuck in Colt's throat. "My wife and I would love to have those pictures. When can I pick them up?"

"I can bring them to you."

"You don't have to."

"Son, you all have been through enough down there. I've got business about ten miles from High Plains. I'll swing by and drop these off at the police station."

"I would really appreciate that." Colt ended the call and then he got out of his car. Their wedding pictures. He wondered if God was in on this.

When he called his sister, he wasn't sure what he wanted to say. She sounded as surprised by the call. They had family dinners from time to time, but life was busy and they didn't get together as much as they should.

He regretted that, along with other things.

"Ang, can we get together for lunch?"

"Of course we can. What's up?"

"I need to talk."

"Well, it's about time." Her words were brightly

spoken, and she laughed a little. "I'll meet you at your place. I'll bring egg salad."

"Angie, I don't like egg salad."

"I thought you loved it?"

"Nope, just didn't want to hurt your feelings."

"I'll bring ham."

"Thanks, sis, you're the best. Could we have lunch here, at the police station?"

"Of course I'm the best, and yes, I'll meet you there." Long pause. "Colt, how is Lexi doing?"

"She's good. She's still sick, but…"

"Are the rumors true? That the two of you were at church together?"

"It doesn't take long to spread the news, does it?"

"Jennifer called."

"Of course she did." His sister's best friend. "I'll see you at noon."

And at noon, she walked through the door of the police station, smiling the way she always smiled. She spoke to the file clerk, Kathleen, and headed back to his office.

"You look pretty bad." She closed the door as she stepped in, and then hugged him.

"Thank you. Words of encouragement are always appreciated."

"Oh, Colt, you're so dry. Try to cheer up."

She opened the bag she had carried in and

pulled out two foil-covered plates. "Ham, dill pickles and potato salad."

Colt offered her a bottle of water out of the fridge. He sat across from her, balancing his plate on his knee. She bowed her head to pray before she ate.

When she finished praying, he met her curious gaze.

"What gives?"

"I'm trying to work through a few things."

"I'm something you have to work through?" Her brows came together and her smile dimmed.

"No, of course not. I'm trying to find my way back to faith. I'm trying to look at things that have happened and see what God has done, not what I think He should have done."

"That isn't easy for a fixer like you, is it?"

"No, but it's my own step one in moving forward."

She smiled, the mom smile he'd seen her use on her kids.

"Colt, you've always taken everything too much to heart. From the puppies we had to give away when you were a kid, to the cows bellowing when it was weaning time for the calves."

"Yeah, maybe." He didn't want to remember that kid, a lot like Tommy, getting attached and now wanting to give up. Which was why Colt kept looking for that dog.

"Colt, you had a yard sale and tried to sell Mom's china because you thought you could save the farm after Dad got hurt."

He had done that. Heat climbed up his cheeks. Big lawman, brought down by his five-foot-three-inch sister. She knew too many of his stories.

"That was one of my finer moments. I can't believe the lady bought the china and then gave it back to Mom."

"You were cute, with your torn jeans and blond hair."

"It bothered me, Angie. It bothered me that you were all laughing and acting as if everything was great, and they were auctioning off part of our farm to pay hospital bills. We went to church and we sang songs about faith. We prayed together at night. And I just couldn't see it."

"You couldn't see that God was getting us through a difficult time? Couldn't you see that we still had Dad, and that our family got stronger, not weaker?"

"Now, yes, I can see that now." And he remembered what Lexi had said about Tommy, losing his dog but gaining a family. All things worked together for good.

"Colt, what in the world is going on with you?"

He looked up, meeting the concern in his sister's gray eyes. "I'm trying to get past what happened, to Dad, to our family and to Gavin. I walked away from my marriage because I kept thinking that given time, I would hurt Lexi—something would happen to her and I wouldn't be able to save her. And then my fear changed to what if we had kids and something happened to me."

"You should have talked to us."

"I can't go back."

"Okay, so move forward and give yourself a break. Try to find faith. Stop having these 'garage sales' where you think you have to save everyone."

"I'm working on it. It isn't easy, though." He smiled. "'Garage sales'?"

"Yeah, you think you have to take care of things, so you take action. Admit it, the yard sale was kind of sweet, but kind of funny."

"Cute. I was looking for words of wisdom."

"I know, and I'm not going to give you platitudes."

"Thank you, I appreciate that. Did you know that Lexi is thinking about moving back to Manhattan?"

"She told you?"

"Not in so many words, no. Jill was the one letting that cat out of the bag."

"Lexi thinks it is time for the two of you to move on. She said her life has been on hold for two years."

"I know." His life had been in the same holding pattern.

A car door slammed. Colt glanced out the window at the truck parked in front of the police station. An older man stepped onto the sidewalk, carrying a box. "There he is."

"Who?"

"Mr. Carlson. I haven't met him but I think that's him." Colt pointed to the farmer in his overalls and work boots. "He found what he believes are our wedding pictures."

"Oh, Colt." Tears trickled down her cheeks.

"Sis, I don't cry easy, but if you do that, I might."

"I'm sorry, but you have to know how special this is. I talked to Lexi after the tornado. She was so torn up over the pictures."

"And her rings?"

"She mentioned it. She wasn't going to tell you."

He reached into his pocket and pulled out the platinum band, circled with diamonds. "I found it in her backyard."

It wasn't often that he could surprise his sister. This did the trick. Her mouth dropped and she blinked a few times. And then she cried for real, wiping her eyes with her napkin.

"I have to see a man about some pictures."

"You haven't told her?"

"Not yet. And don't you tell. I'm working through this and I'm praying, Ang. These rings mean something, but that's something else I'm working on."

He placed the rings on the table in front of her. She picked them up and held them to the light. "Not a scratch on them."

"Not one." He took them from her outstretched hand and put them into his pocket.

He walked out the door of his office and greeted the farmer who had found his wedding photographs. "Here they are, son. Now, they're not perfect. Some of them are a little torn. The book got wet and there are water stains."

"I don't think she'll be worried about that." Colt opened the bag and pulled out the wedding album. The floral design was ripped away from the binding and the water damage had peeled away some of the pages.

He opened the book to the photograph of the two of them together. Newlyweds, still believing marriage was forever. He remembered that day, and how he had imagined their lives together.

"I take it they're yours?"

Colt nodded, still a little stunned. He hadn't looked at these pictures in a long time. The images brought back a wash of memories, good memories of feeling in love and knowing they could make it through anything.

And then regret, because he hadn't fought hard enough to make it over the biggest obstacle, his own pride. As he flipped through the pages, he landed on one photograph. Lexi's dad at their reception. He was on his phone, probably taking care of business. Lexi stood next to him, and her smile looked as if it was about to melt away.

He slipped that photograph from the book and stuck it in his pocket. He hadn't planned on being like her dad, always putting her somewhere at the back of the line. But that's exactly what he had done.

The man standing next to Colt cleared his throat.

"Well, I should be going. I have a load of calves to get home."

"Thank you for this." Colt shook a worn and weathered hand, gnarled by arthritis.

"Don't mention it. I would have wanted the same done for me."

Angie walked out the door, her purse over her shoulder. She stopped next to him. "I'm going home, but I want you to know that there's a purpose in all of this, so don't get lost in all of the whys, trying to make sense of it. Do what you feel is right."

"At this point, I have no idea what that is."

"I think you do." She hugged him and then she walked away and he wished he could smile as easily as she did. She had never lost faith.

## Chapter Eleven

The two little girls ran toward Lexi as she came out of the grocery store. She still wasn't feeling great, but she knew she wasn't contagious, and the girls looked as if they had something to discuss. She waited for them, glancing around the area for any sight of the feuding parents of the two children—Alyssa's aunt, Josie Cane, and Lilli's father, Silas Marstow. If she could have, Lexi would have explained to the two adults that they were both good parents. They probably didn't want to hear from her that they should cut one another a little slack.

"Hi, girls."

"Hello." Alyssa looked around, fidgeting and scrunching the hem of her shirt.

"Shouldn't you be at the day care?" Lexi squatted to the level of the two girls.

"I should be," Alyssa whispered, "but I saw Lilli waiting for her dad. He's talking to someone. And he'll talk a long time."

"I see."

"Ask her, Alyssa, ask her what it means for someone to be damaged goods. That's what I heard someone say about Miss Josie. They said she has a past," Lilli whispered, looking around as she spoke.

"Oh, honey, where in the world did you hear that?" Lexi wanted to know so she could give that someone a piece of her mind. Josie Cane probably had mistakes in her past like anyone else, but Lexi didn't believe anyone was damaged goods.

"I can't tell." Lilli started to squirm. "We want a puppy. We think it would be a good making-up gift for my dad and Miss Josie. If she thought he brought it to her, she'd be real happy."

"Girls, you can't do that." But it was a sweet idea. "You can get the grown-ups to come in and talk to me about some puppies that I have, but I can't let you take one without adult permission."

"How do we get adult permission?" Alyssa stepped forward, taking Lexi by the hand.

"I'm not sure, but together we'll think of something. We need to find a way to get them to come in together."

"I have an idea." Lilli twirled her skirt and a

smile spread across her tiny face. What a precious child. And Lexi wondered how she remained so happy, with Silas always so thunderous.

Footsteps on the sidewalk. Lexi and the girls looked up, expecting Silas. It was Colt. Lexi felt a moment of relief that was short-lived.

"Lilli Marstow, your dad is looking for you. You'd better scoot on back down there. Alyssa, kiddo, let me walk you across the street."

"What about me?" Lexi stood, waiting for instructions.

Colt winked. Oh, she loved him. She wasn't about to admit how much, but at moments like this, it was nearly too much. How could she stay in town, feeling that way about a man who only wanted to work on getting along when they had to be around each other?

"You wait." He had hold of Alyssa's hand. The two—tall cop in his dark T-shirt that said Police across the chest and the little girl—walked across the street.

He waited on the other side and watched as Alyssa ran back to the day care and then he crossed to where Lexi waited. She watched him walking toward her, carrying a plastic bag that he held up as he got closer.

"I have a surprise for you."

"Really." She reached for the bag, but he pulled it back.

"This is a really special surprise."

"Okay." She tried to make out the form hidden by the bag. "What is it?"

"You're very impatient." He slipped an arm through hers. "I think we should go back to my office, Lexi."

"Am I in trouble?"

"Not yet." His grin changed from charming to a little wicked. "But you might be."

"Say it isn't so." Her heart thumped against her ribs.

"It is." He held her close to his side. "People are watching. They're going to spread rumors."

"Small-town life. Don't you love it?" And she wanted him to always tease this way, the way he had when they had first met.

"I do." He opened the door to the police station. "Ladies first."

"Thank you." But her insides were shifting, nervous, upset. She didn't know if it was the food poisoning or anticipation—or fear.

He had always done this to her. When they were dating, he was constantly bringing surprises. She missed that Colt, the surprising Colt. He had disappeared three or four years ago.

She had been thinking a lot about why she had let him walk away. There were probably several reasons. But he was next to her, and his tender gaze wouldn't let her remain in thoughts of the past.

They walked into his office and he closed the door behind them. They were alone. She didn't know if alone was a good idea.

"Stop looking so upset." He kissed her cheek. "This isn't a bad thing."

She nodded, but then she blurted it out, "I've missed you like this."

Her words surprised him. She saw the change in his expression, from happiness to something that resembled sorrow. His smile faded and his eyes softened. He pulled her close, nuzzling her cheek and holding her as if he might hold her forever, holding her as if it might take away the pain.

"I didn't mean to leave you alone." He kissed her, his lips grazing hers, and then lingering. His hands, strong and warm, cupped her face. She melted into his embrace for a kiss that took her back in time, to when they were in love and believed in forever.

Before love got so difficult and their grasp on forever slipped away.

"Stop." She whispered as she backed away. "We can't do this."

"You're right. One step at a time. Right now, we're working on friendship."

"And then what?"

"I don't know. I thought we needed to work on friendship so that the two of us could move forward, move on with our lives."

"Okay, so this is part of a process? Step one in moving on?"

"Isn't that what you're doing? Aren't you planning to move back to Manhattan?"

"I don't know. I guess I've thought about it. This was my home, with you. But now, I don't know anymore."

"This is more complicated than I thought it would be."

She sat down on the edge of his desk. "You know, when I think of our marriage ending, I'm always trying to put my finger on why. There are marriages that fall apart for a reason, Colt. I've known women who were physically abused. They reached deep down and found the strength to leave."

He sat down next to her and she laced her fingers through his. "Lex, I know those women, too. I know those families— being apart for them is safer than being together."

"But what happened to us? I've been trying to figure out why I let you leave. I think letting you go was easier than fighting to keep you in my life. I've had a lifetime of searching for ways to involve my parents in my life. I didn't want my marriage to be a repeat. After a while that gets to a girl's self-esteem. It makes her wonder what is wrong with her that she has to fight to make people love her."

"I didn't mean to make you feel that way. It wasn't about you, not really. It was about guilt, and then about keeping you safe, and then fear."

"I get it. That doesn't make it any easier." She held her hand out to the bag he had set on the other side of the desk. "I'd like to see that now."

He handed it over. She pulled the album from the bag and emotion clogged her throat, tightening in her chest and squeezing her heart.

"Our wedding pictures."

"I got a call today from a man who found them in his field. He wasn't sure where to take them, and then he saw me on the news."

"Amazing." She flipped through pages. "I can't believe it."

"God does amazing things."

She glanced up, briefly, and then back down at the book. Pictures of them walking down the aisle, and then eating cake. She laughed a little at the two of them, so young and so in love. He had been her everything. Maybe that had been the problem. She had counted on him to fix her life.

Now she knew better. She knew better than to think a person could be that for her. He had been a part of the dream, one of the ingredients she thought made up a happy life. She had made him her everything.

"I prayed that someone would find them. I couldn't bear to lose this." She flipped through more pages.

"I didn't realize."

"I know it doesn't make sense."

"It does. It makes perfect sense." He pulled her against his side and kissed the top of her head. His radio crackled.

Lexi looked up as he stepped away. He spoke quietly into the mic and then listened. He nodded, as if the person could see him. As he spoke, he unlocked the cabinet that held his weapons. Fear walloped her heart as she watched him load a weapon and retrieve a box of ammunition.

"Lexi, I'm sorry. I have to go."

"I know."

He kissed her cheek. "You know this doesn't mean that I'm leaving you."

"I know." She picked up the album. "I'm taking this home with me."

"Of course. I'll stop by later." He stopped at the door. "Lexi, I've been thinking about something. Did you love me, or was it having a family that you loved?"

"Colt." But his words, hard as they were to hear, made her stop, made her think. Hadn't she just been thinking the same thing, that he was one ingredient, one item on the list that she thought she needed to have a happy life? She could remember the first time she went home with him, to meet his family.

"That's something to think about." He walked out the door and left her alone.

She watched his car back out of the parking space. Like so many other times, she prayed he'd stay safe. She also prayed for him to have faith. Something in his eyes, a certain light, told her that the faith part was being answered.

Her cell phone buzzed and she answered it. What she needed was a call that would take her mind off Colt. And this one did. A cow having birthing issues. That was always a good way to spend an afternoon. She didn't mind it on a nice fall day, like today. The middle of the night in a storm, or the dead of winter, that was another matter.

As she drove down the side road that led past her house, she flipped on the scanner hooked to the dash of her truck. And she shouldn't have, because it wasn't good. They had Parsons located in an abandoned house, just a mile or so outside of High Plains.

And Colt was on his way to the scene.

Colt pulled up to Lexi's as the sun was going down. He got out of his truck, stretching muscles that were sore from being tense for so many hours as they worked through the standoff with Parsons. He was only starting to come down from the adrenaline and fear that came from gunfire. But Parsons was in custody now.

As he crossed the drive, he realized Lexi's truck wasn't there. He peeked through the window of the front door, into the darkened clinic and tiny apartment. Not one light, no sign of anyone.

He pulled out his cell phone and dialed her number. She answered on the third ring.

"Where are you?"

"Hello to you, too." She laughed a little. "Sorry, I didn't realize I had to check in with you."

He had a moment that hit like a physical blow, somewhere in the region of his stomach, or maybe his heart. It was just past dinnertime and she wasn't home. What if she was on a date? They had both dated some in the last year or so. They weren't married. She was single and beautiful.

He was jealous.

Maybe this had something to do with the question he'd asked her about his family. That thought had been on his mind too much. He should have kept it to himself.

"Colt, are you there?"

"Yes, I'm here. Sorry, I didn't mean to bother you. I'll call tomorrow."

"You're not bothering me. I'm downtown, having dinner. I had a call and on the way home, I stopped at Walter's farm. A few people were there patching his roof. I'm getting very good at roofing. If the whole veterinarian thing doesn't work out, I have another skill. And they put the roof on the Old Town Hall today."

"Do you really think we can call it the Old Town Hall? It's the Old Town Hall twice removed, maybe?"

She laughed. "Yes, maybe. Are you okay?"

"We caught Parsons."

A long pause. "I'm glad. I'm glad you're safe."

He walked toward the building that was meant to be her new home.

"Was your contractor here today?" He picked up a hammer that had been left in the dirt and placed it on a pile of wood.

"Nope. I think he worked at Melanie and Ted's new house."

"Lexi, I don't know…"

"Don't, Colt. Take a few hours off from being a cop and come down here and have coffee and cheesecake with us. We're all here, at Isabella's, trying to pretend life is normal and that half the town isn't living at the cottages, or elsewhere."

"Can I wait for you here? I'm a little too wound up for company."

"Sure."

He said goodbye and slipped his phone back into his pocket. Instead of sitting outside the clinic he walked down the street, still amazed that this used to be his town. Trees were now piles of firewood, waiting for winter. Houses that had stood for decades were now empty foundations. People he'd known his entire life had left to start their lives over again in new towns, with new jobs and new homes.

A few blocks down, he saw Nicki Appleton walking with Kasey. From the distance the child looked as if she belonged to Nicki. He would have liked for that to happen for her. Maybe Kasey would replace the holes in her heart, left behind by Clay Logan.

Colt shook his head and turned away from the sight of Nicki and Kasey. It brought to mind holes in his own heart, the place where his wife should be. He walked back to her house, questioning why he was there. They had made progress in the friendship department. Maybe it was time to take a step back and continue the moving on part of the process?

Lexi's truck was parked next to the clinic. She was just getting out, her smile wide, and for him. He pulled the photograph, bent and water-stained, from his pocket. The picture of her father talking on his cell phone.

\* \* \*

This was too much like the past. Lexi couldn't get around the feelings that her life had somehow come full circle. She was waiting outside for Colt. He was in his uniform.

He thought she might have married him for his family.

"Hey, how did it go?" She didn't want details, didn't want to know if he'd been in danger. It was easier not knowing.

"Good. He gave up." He smiled, a little tense, and shrugged. She knew that Parsons hadn't given up, not without a fight.

This was the past, too. He gave few details, because he didn't want her to worry. He had never shared details, not real ones, about the night Gavin died. He had kept it bottled up inside.

"Do you want something to eat?" She lifted a bag with takeout. "Isabella's world-famous spaghetti."

He laughed. "How do you think spaghetti from High Plains became 'world famous'?"

"A guy visiting from England. He had a cousin that lived outside of town. And once, a man traveling through was from Spain. That's two countries, and that makes up the world as far as Isabella is concerned."

She unlocked her front door and motioned him

inside. He took the bag and handed her a photograph. Lexi looked at it, and then at him, because she didn't get it. A picture of her dad on the phone?

"That was a photograph from our wedding." He opened the container and stirred the sauce into the pasta. "Lexi, he was on the phone. He couldn't turn it off, not even for that one day."

She shrugged, trying not to be hurt by that. She had seen it that day, but had forgotten. And it hadn't really mattered; her dad had never really been present in her life, not in a way that mattered.

"Colt, I'm sorry, if this is supposed to mean something, I'm not getting it. Maybe it's just been a long day."

He poured a glass of tea and lifted the pitcher. "Do you want tea?"

She shook her head. No, she wanted the mystery revealed. She wanted him out of her kitchen, where it was too familiar, him offering to pour her tea, the two of them discussing something that felt like one of his cases.

It hurt too much, having him there, as if they still belonged together. And they didn't.

"He put his job ahead of your happiness." Colt pulled out a chair at the table and motioned for her to sit. She didn't. She couldn't sit.

"Keep talking."

"Okay." He sat down, sliding the tray of food

in front of him. "Lexi, in ways, I became like your father. I got so wrapped up in my job, in answering calls, I forgot about us."

That hurt. It ached deep down, and for a few minutes she felt like that little girl whose father never showed up for her birthday. But it was Colt, and he had promised to always be there for her.

Her father probably felt as though he was always there. He had provided a beautiful home, all the toys and pretty clothes she could ask for. And he had never been there for her when she'd needed him. Not even on her wedding.

He had been on the phone, taking care of a client, taking care of business. She could almost hear him say what he always said: *It's business, Lexi, and business pays the bills. This business is what puts this roof over your head and affords you all the nice things you like.*

He hadn't gotten it, that she would have preferred time with him to the things he bought to replace that time.

"Maybe I have unrealistic expectations." She finally sat down.

"I think we should be able to expect the people in our lives to be there for us."

"Yes, but things come up. We do have jobs. There were times I had to leave in the middle of dinner because of a horse or cow or dog."

"You didn't let your job steal your life." He looked down, twirling pasta around his fork. "I let it consume me."

"I agree, you did. And you let it come between us."

"What if…"

"Don't, Colt, I don't want to do this because we're both emotional right now." She shook her head. "I don't want 'what ifs' from you. I want someone who will be there for me in a way that counts, not closed off, sleeping on the sofa and choosing his office over my bed."

"I didn't want you to be hurt the way Gavin's wife was."

"We were going to have a baby, Colt. And then you decided we weren't. You made that decision for me. I can't go through that again."

"I know you can't. And I know I took the easy way out." He looked up, his blue eyes meeting hers, holding her gaze. "I did what I thought would protect your heart, because I know how much having children means to you. I took the easy way for myself and I'm sorry."

The wedding album was on the table between them. She opened it and pointed to the photograph of the two of them standing in front of the minister. "To have and to hold, good times and bad. And we gave up the minute things got rough.

Did you think marriage would be this free ride, easy, no rough patches to work through?"

He shrugged. "Do you know that my parents never fought in front of us?"

"And?" Now he was losing her. This was about them, their marriage.

"I really thought that was the way marriage worked. You got along, and sometimes you didn't talk, but you also didn't work through everything."

Lexi didn't hide the giggle that sneaked up on her. She reached for his hand. "Poor Colt, you didn't know how to deal with a wife that wanted to talk it all out. Your parents fought—they just worked it out when you weren't listening. Or they let it go."

"Michael suggested we talk to him together." His face, golden tan from the summer, turned a little red.

"We could do that."

"We could." He flipped through the album. She thought he would say more, about them, about the future, but he didn't. And she wondered if talking to Michael was just another way for them to move on. Or something else. And she didn't want to hope.

But there it was anyway, hope, rising up in her heart, probably showing on her face as if she was a giddy teenager waiting for a date to the prom.

He stood and reached for her hand. His thumb rubbed her fingers. "I should probably go."

"Yes, you probably should. And thank you for bringing this." She ran her hand over the photo album. "It means so much."

He saluted as he walked away, two fingers to his brow. Her heart melted.

## Chapter Twelve

Lexi walked along the narrow dirt road, looking for signs of Charlie. She didn't know why, but the dog wouldn't leave her mind. Maybe because she'd seen the posters in town, replaced again. Please Help Me Find Charlie read one poster. It broke her heart, bringing back too many childhood memories of wanting her own dog to come home.

A car slowed to a stop next to her. She turned, smiling at Josie Cane, Alyssa's unsuspecting aunt. Poor Josie, she had no idea the girls were trying to patch things up between her and Silas.

"Hi, Lexi." Josie, blond and pretty, leaned out the window.

"Good morning." Lexi glanced back in the direction Josie had driven from. "You're still at the cottages?"

"Still there. Sometimes I wonder if life will ever get back to normal."

"I don't know if normal exists." Lexi walked up out of the ditch. "I'm out here looking for Charlie. That dog has to be somewhere."

"Speaking of dogs."

Lexi knew what was coming. "I have newborn puppies. They won't be ready for at least another six weeks or so."

"I want to make sure she understands that a puppy is a lot of responsibility."

"In a few weeks they'll be bigger. You could bring her over and show her how to care for them. Maybe she could help out around the clinic and feed some of the animals for me. I can give her housebreaking tips."

"Do you mind, because that would be great?"

"I think we could arrange it." Lexi smiled, as if it was about Josie volunteering, and not the exceptional planning of two little girls. She liked being in on something with those two. Whatever plan the girls came up with, Lexi knew that the outcome would be great.

"Great. Well, I need to get to work. I'll call, soon."

Lexi nodded and stepped back as Josie drove away.

And still no sign of Charlie. She walked back to her truck, saying a little prayer that if the dog was alive, he'd come back. Tommy would survive without the animal. She knew that. But the dog meant so much to him.

Another vehicle was heading her way. She stepped to the back of her truck and waited for Colt's Jeep to slow down and stop. He pushed dark sunglasses back on his head and leaned out the window.

"What are you doing out here?" She walked up to his window, and she remembered days when she would have leaned in to kiss him, when she had the right to do that.

"I was looking for you." He peered past her. "What are you doing out here?"

"Looking for Charlie. I don't know. I just thought maybe he'd be here, somewhere near water and people. I used to see him out here, hunting in the field."

Her phone buzzed at her side. She ignored it and let it go to voice mail. It rang again.

"You'd better take that."

"Yeah, I know." She flipped it open, smiling as she moved it to her ear.

"Lexi, you have to get into town, quick. It's your house." Mayor Dawson, out of breath, her voice breaking up. "Honey, your house is on fire."

"I'll be right there." Chills ran through her body and her vision clouded. Colt's hand was on her arm.

"What's wrong?"

"My house. My house is on fire." She looked at her phone. "I don't know if they mean my clinic or the house. I have animals in there, Colt."

His radio crackled as the call came in, asking the fire department to respond to a structure fire. Colt grabbed his radio and broke in, asking Bud to give him more information.

"I'm heading that way." Lexi started to move but he had hold of her arm.

"Get in. You can't drive like this. I'll send someone out here to get your truck."

Lexi agreed, she couldn't drive. She climbed in next to him, and Colt hit the siren and lights as they accelerated and headed for High Plains.

She could see the smoke and she prayed, really prayed, that her animals were okay. And then she remembered the photo album that Colt had brought to her. She had just gotten it back. She didn't want to lose it again.

The information Colt had asked for came over the radio. It was her house, not her clinic. And someone had broken into the clinic to get her animals out to safety, in case the fire spread.

"What am I going to do?"

"Start over." Colt made it sound easy. In a soothing voice, it sounded logical. Start over.

"I'm tired of starting over."

"You don't know the full extent of the damage.

Wait until we see what is going on before you make a decision."

"I know." She leaned against the window, her attention focused on the trail of smoke coming from her house. "This is when it is hard to find faith. Or maybe this is God telling me something."

"Maybe." Colt slowed as they entered town. "Lexi, I'm not going to let you lose it on this one. I know you've been through a lot, but this isn't the end."

"Just another beginning. Yeah, I know. I'm tired of beginnings. I want to be settled. I thought that at this point in my life I'd be..."

She couldn't finish. He was waiting, she knew he was, but she wouldn't hurt either of them with what would sound like accusations. They both shared responsibility in their failed marriage.

Colt turned onto her road, stopping a short distance from the house. The yard was crowded with fire trucks, and people stood at the edge of the street.

"I know what you thought." His hand on her arm stopped her from getting out of the Jeep. "At this point in your life, you thought you'd be married, have a home and a couple of kids. You didn't see yourself divorced, starting over by yourself."

"No, you're right, that isn't how the story was supposed to go. But I'm not blaming you."

"If that's supposed to make me feel better, it doesn't. I do blame myself."

She closed her eyes and took a deep breath. "I have to check on my house."

But there was no house left. She got out of the Jeep and walked across the road to the crowd of people. The firemen were still spraying the smoldering spots, but it hadn't taken long for the framed house to burn to the ground.

"This is unbelievable." Her contractor walked up. "Lexi, I'm sorry. I don't know what to say. They think the fire came from the connection on the pole. Something sparked. I don't know."

"Don't worry about it. This is just round three and tomorrow I'll tackle this. I'll decide what to do."

"I'll stay, to make sure things get cleaned up," he offered.

"Thank you, I'd appreciate that." In a daze she walked away from the burned-out foundation, back to the metal building that housed her clinic and her temporary home.

Colt stayed behind to talk. When he jogged to her side, she turned, expecting soft words to brush off her pain. Instead he just shrugged. "I don't know how to make this better."

"You could say this is a horrible dream."

His smile was gentle and sweet. "I wish I could."

"I know. Don't worry, I'm down but not defeated.

This is another bump in the road, but I need a day or two to lick my wounds. I'm going to go inside, feel sorry for myself, cry for an hour or so, and tomorrow I'll be back to having faith."

"Do you want me to stay?"

Oh, boy, did she. She shook her head. "No, that's okay."

Because she had learned to stand on her own two feet. She didn't want to get back into the habit of relying on him for her stability. Tonight she needed to really think about her future.

Colt made a loop through the area around the Waters cottages, still hoping for something that might lead to information on Kasey's family. The little girl wasn't old enough to give them information. He had nothing to go on.

And not one clue pointing in the direction of parents, family or how she came to be in High Plains.

He disliked that deep-seated feeling of having failed. He had failed this little girl. She was still unknown, without parents, without a past. And he couldn't do one thing about it.

As he drove back into High Plains, he saw Michael's car and pulled in next to it. Michael got out of his car and walked up to Colt's open driver's-side window.

"I thought maybe you'd had enough of me," Michael teased.

"I like torture." Colt leaned over the steering wheel of the Jeep and stared out the windshield, trying to make sense of what felt like a huge puzzle.

"What's up?"

"I can't help that little girl. I can't find Charlie. Lexi's house is nothing but a black spot on the ground."

"You can't do it all, Colt. Try prayer. Let God have a hand at some of these situations you're trying to solve on your own."

"I'm not good at sitting back and waiting."

He wanted to fix the situations, not wait for answers that might not come, or might not be the answers they wanted.

"One thing at a time, Colt. One day at a time."

"Good advice, my friend."

"Glad I could help. Oh, Walter has a house that is ready for winter, thanks to you. That's one thing taken care of."

Colt nodded. "Thanks for helping out with that."

"No problem. I'll see you later, I have a date with Heather."

Colt shifted into Reverse and backed out of the parking space. He could see Tommy in front of Greg Garrison's office. It hadn't taken the businessman long to get his life and office back in order.

Tommy waved, and Colt pulled over. The boy ran up to the car, his smile hopeful. "Have you seen Charlie?"

"No, Tommy, I haven't." Colt sighed. "But I'm praying we can find him."

He was praying. How long had it been since he'd gone in that direction? But the little boy was smiling, his pain maybe a little less intense after two months.

"Yeah, me, too. But I was hoping you could help."

"I'm not going to stop looking," Colt assured him. Maya appeared at the door of the office. "Hey, I think Maya wants you to come inside. Tommy, God did some great things in your life. You know that, right?"

The little boy nodded. "Yeah, I know. I'm learning about being thankful in Sunday school. But I sure miss my dog."

"I bet you do. I'll keep an eye out for Charlie. I know Dr. Harmon has been looking for him, too."

"Yeah, I know."

Tommy skipped away, back to the office, and Maya.

Colt cruised on, past buildings that would never be the same. But some were coming back, slowly but surely. It felt good to see what they'd accomplished in the two months since the tornado. He slowed down to look at the gazebo, now just an empty spot, no grass and a few concrete blocks. Cleaned up, but not rebuilt. It was on the list of things to rebuild, but it was at the bottom of the list.

An unfamiliar car drove past him. He glanced, and then took a second look. His ex-mother-in-law. He groaned and turned to follow her back to Lexi's clinic.

She was out of her car when he pulled up. "Colt, how are you?"

She looked every inch the successful Realtor that she was. From the sleek hair, to clothes that never wrinkled, she had the look. He'd heard her one too many times criticize Lexi for not taking more care with her personal appearance.

"I'm fine, Anita. Lexi's on a call."

"I realize that. But my question is, why are you back in my daughter's life?"

"We're friends, Anita. We can't live in the past."

"You know she's miserable with you. She was miserable when she thought she was having your baby, and you left her."

His world went cold and he sucked in a deep breath. "What in the world are you talking about?"

"If you'd been there, you would know."

"I have to go."

"Is that how you worked through your marriage, Colt, by walking away?"

"If I'm going to talk, I'll talk to Lexi."

"And if I have my way, she won't be here much longer. I've found her a darling little house with a nice lot and an office attached."

"In Manhattan?"

She nodded, lifting brochures for him to see. "With her family."

The word was empty when Anita said it. *Family.* To her, it meant only that she'd have won control of Lexi. Or so she thought.

But he couldn't have that conversation with Anita, not when her words were still slipping through his mind, mocking him. Lexi had thought she was pregnant. And he had left her.

She hadn't said anything.

Lexi gave the last calf its immunization and stretched. Her back ached, her legs ached, and if she thought about it, her arms did, too. Twenty calves, a few ornery steers that had to be dealt with, and then that goat. The Stalwarts had a great operation, but they always seemed to save everything up for one day.

The tornado hadn't been easy on them, either. They'd lost one barn and part of their hay for winter. Last week a rancher from Oklahoma had shown up with a load of round bales, free.

She walked back to her truck and wrote up a bill that Jason Stalwart would grumble about and then write a check for, because he knew her rates were some of the best in the county, and because days after getting out of the hospital, she'd been out here, caring for animals that had been injured. And she hadn't charged him.

He knew he could call at any time and she'd be there. She smiled as she handed him his copy of the bill.

"You've got to be kidding." He shook his head. "What is this world coming to?"

"Well, for one thing, Jason, you'll have healthy calves that you can sell next year. You have a goat that isn't going to die. Your kids can keep showing that ornery angus steer." She smiled at him. "Should I go on?"

He pulled his checkbook out of the front pocket of his bib overalls. "I think you've said enough."

"You know you appreciate me."

"Yeah, I appreciate you. I'm just glad you don't hold a gun to my head when you rob me this way."

Mrs. Stalwart walked up, wiping her hands on a kitchen towel. "Jason, stop giving her such a hard time. Lexi, he only does that because he likes you."

"Don't tell her all of my secrets." He tore off the check and handed it to her. "There you go. Mom, you're going to have to go easy on the shopping for a few days."

Mrs. Stalwart slapped him with a towel. "Get in

the house and wash up for supper. Lexi, do you want to stay for meatballs?"

"No, I can't. My mother is in town waiting for me."

"Oh, I hope we didn't keep you too long."

Not long enough. Lexi smiled and shook her head. "No, you didn't. I'll see you at church on Sunday."

"Lexi, is Colt okay?"

Lexi turned. "Okay?"

"Well, they said that man shot at him the other day."

"Shot at him?"

"You didn't know." Mrs. Stalwart bit down on her bottom lip. "Oh, honey, I'm sorry for opening my big mouth."

"I had no idea. But he's fine." And still hiding things from her. So much for friendship and putting the past behind them.

It hurt worse because she had allowed herself to believe they were becoming more than friends. Something in his eyes, in the way he touched her, made her believe he might still love her.

Had they ever really stopped loving one another?

Lexi drove home, thinking about Colt, thinking about her mother, and thinking about how everyone seemed to want to make decisions for her. Including her ex-husband, who was still deciding what she could handle and what she couldn't.

And it made her mad.

When she pulled into the drive of her clinic, her mother was sitting at the picnic table, waiting. And she didn't look happy. It was sunny. The shade trees were gone. The doors were locked.

Lexi parked and got out. She hesitated at her truck, thinking that she could always leave. She could tell her mom that she didn't have to listen to this, and that she had business to take care of with Colt. Instead she sat down at the picnic table, stained hands clasped in front of her.

"Mom, good to see you."

"Lexi, you're going to love what I have to show you."

"Mom, not right now."

"What does that mean? I thought you had your mind made up?" Anita spread the papers on the table for Lexi to look at. "Look at these places. Especially this one, with the little Cape Cod, the workshop that could be turned into a clinic and this sweet little flower garden."

"It's very lovely, Mom, but there's a place here that I'm interested in. It's a nice three-bedroom craftsman style, with land, and I already have a clinic."

"What about your insurance money? The fire

had to take a good chunk. How will you buy when you lost so much?"

"I'm not in as bad a shape as some of the people around here."

"Fine, I get that, but I drove over here to show you these properties because you asked."

Lexi sighed. "Okay, I'll look at the houses, but you have to give me room to breathe. I'm going to make this decision on my own."

Her mom smiled, pleased and thinking she had won. Lexi skimmed over the properties that two hours ago she wouldn't have considered. Now she had to consider them, and her future. Colt had been shot at, and he hadn't bothered to tell her.

Colt drove past Lexi's three times and on the fourth trip down her street, her mom's car was gone. He pulled in and parked next to Lexi's truck. He didn't get out. Instead he sat in his Jeep and looked at her house.

He didn't know what he was going to say to her. He couldn't go in, accusing her of keeping things from him. Not when he had things he'd kept to himself.

For three hours he'd been beating himself up, because he hadn't been there for her. But then again, she had very carefully closed him out during those last six months of their marriage. She had distanced herself and so had he.

Colt walked up to the front door and she opened it before he could knock. Her nose flared and her eyes narrowed. She crossed her arms and stared, and he was the one that was taken by surprise. He had planned on being the one doing the confronting, not the one feeling defensive.

That look did it, though. He took a step back and nearly apologized before she told him why she was mad.

"You should have told me." Her brows arched and her head tilted, waiting for an answer to an accusation he didn't get.

"What should I have told you? Maybe we should talk about things you should have told me."

"I tried to get you to let me in, to share what you were going through. What else could I have said?"

"You could have told me you were pregnant." He lowered his voice and took another step, leaning against the door frame, wanting her to walk into his arms.

She didn't. Instead she sighed and shook her head. "I was never pregnant. I wouldn't have kept that from you. No matter what."

A catch in her voice told the story that her words wouldn't tell. He moved, wanting to pull her close, but he didn't. He wasn't ready, and from the steely look in her eyes, she wasn't looking for someone to comfort her.

"Your mom said…"

Lexi shook her head. Her lips pursed and her nose turned pink. She didn't cry. "I thought I was pregnant, but I wasn't. I was happy, sad, I don't know, about a million emotions that I can't begin to explain to you."

"I think I understand." Because even now, thinking of her having his child did unexpected things to his heart, to his brain. And thinking that they might never have a family, that twisted other emotions.

He came to terms with one fact: that he wanted more than friendship with her. He wanted her back in his life.

He wanted to hit something. He wanted to hold her close and tell her they could work this out. He wanted to scream to God that this wasn't fair, because it shouldn't hurt so much to love someone, to want to give them everything and to be afraid of taking more than that, leaving them with nothing.

"You didn't tell me Parsons shot at you," she whispered and tears did fill her eyes, spilling out on her sunburned cheeks.

"I didn't want you to worry."

"I can deal with worry, Colt. I can't deal with

you hiding things from me. I can't deal with you not trusting me to be strong and to have faith. That's something that has changed in the last two years. I'm a stronger person. I have stronger faith."

"I know you're strong."

"So, we're back to square one, back to you trying so hard to protect me that you pull away from me."

"Maybe, I don't know."

"I still love you."

He had never felt so gut-stomped in his life. He sucked in a deep breath and closed his eyes, thinking how that felt, to hear those words again after so many years. How right it felt.

And how much it scared him.

"Lexi…"

"No, I'm not asking you to say something. I'm not trying to put you on the spot. I just wanted you to know that I can't be *just* a friend."

"Okay, that's fair." And now what? Where did he go from here? "What do we do now?"

With feelings that weren't over and done with?

"I don't know, Colt. I can't do this anymore, trying to be your friend and knowing that there are still walls between us."

Clear blue eyes stared at him, waiting for his answer. Friendship. He had been fooling himself, too. Calling it friendship had been a safe way for him to be in her life again.

"Lexi, how do we go back?"

"I'm not asking you to go back. I'm telling you that I'm moving forward."

"You're going back to Manhattan?" This was coming at him too fast to think the rational thoughts he needed, the words that would have pleaded for her to stay, to give them a second chance.

She didn't want a second chance at the same old thing. He didn't have to ask her to know how true that was. Him, his job, it was still who he was.

When she nodded, he wasn't surprised.

"Yes, I'm thinking about moving back to Manhattan. I don't know what else to do at this point. I've changed, Colt."

"And you think I haven't."

"Have you?"

He took a step back from her doorway. "I don't know. I'm still me. I'm still a cop. And I still wouldn't want anything to hurt you."

"Those aren't bad things, Colt."

"Maybe not. But I don't know if I can be the man you need me to be." He turned and walked away, but she was in the doorway, the light of her living room behind her, and he kept thinking of Gavin on that moonless night, and Gavin's wife, stoic as tears coursed their way down her cheeks.

## Chapter Thirteen

"This can't be the end." Jill tossed the romance novel on the table in front of them and turned to look at Lexi. "I thought you said it was good?"

"It was sort of good. At least it has a happy ending."

"Yeah, the heroine in that book wasn't stubborn and intent on driving the love of her life out of her life. Of course they got together in the end and had their happy-ever-after."

"Is there a point in that statement?"

Jill put her feet up on the coffee table and made a face.

"Of course there's a point. My point is that you and Colt are both stubborn, and you both have to learn to give a little and see each other's side of this love story."

"Thank you, Dr. Jill."

Jill laughed. "You're so welcome. Remember to pay when you receive my bill."

"I'll buy your supper instead. Let's go to Isabella's." Lexi stood up, needing a change of pace and a change of subject.

"Isabella's is closed. They're having an electrical problem."

"Pizza?" Lexi would have eaten dirt to change the subject.

"No, I'm pizza'd out."

"Oh, come on, Jill." Lexi sat back down. "Let's do something."

"I want to talk about those real estate magazines on the coffee table."

"They show houses for sale." Lexi picked up one of the magazines. "Very pretty homes."

"You don't want one of those."

"I know I don't. I want that little house a mile east of town, the one that has a covered front porch, a fenced yard and five acres."

"A swing in the backyard and a little playhouse."

"I want it for the land and the covered porch."

Jill laughed and jerked the magazine out of Lexi's hand. She swatted Lexi on the arm with the rolled-up paper. "You want a happy ending. You want Colt to walk through the door and tell you he'll do all of the right things."

"Would that be so bad?"

"No one ever does *all* of the right things, Lex. That only happens in daydreams of fourteen-year-olds. You could ditch Colt and find something that looks better from the outside, but then you'll realize that the replacement has problems, too." Jill smiled big. "Like computers, you know, we constantly get new updated programs. But each year, when the updates are complete, there are still problems. It's like you trade one glitch for another."

"So, what you're saying is that they all stink, leave dirty clothes on the floor and forget to wash their coffee cup?"

"Exactly. And they all have something that is going to drive us crazy. Colt is a worrier. But he's been in church for the last couple of weeks. He's trying to have faith."

"I know." Lexi glanced down at the listings of homes for sale. "I don't really want to leave."

"Then don't. If you stay, that doesn't mean working things out with Colt. Or maybe it does. But don't go."

"Because you'd miss me?" Lexi teased.

"A lot of people would miss you."

"I would miss it here, but I don't think I can stay and do this friendship thing with Colt. This is a small town and we're always going to be around each other. I don't know how to stay here and watch him go on with his life with someone else."

"Take time, Lexi. Pray about this."

"Let's go do something. There are a few teams from church that are working on houses in town, helping with repairs that insurance wouldn't cover."

"It's six o'clock."

"They're putting up lights and working late. It's supposed to rain in a few days and they want to get some work done before that happens."

"You're serious?" Jill reached for her shoes. "What about eating?"

"We can make a sandwich."

"This is about avoiding dealing with your feelings for Colt, right?"

"My feelings have never been a secret, Jill." Lexi smiled, because this *was* a move to leave the conversation behind.

"Okay, let's go. What do you have in the fridge?" Jill was already crossing the room and opening the door to peek in at the contents. "Smoked turkey?"

"Sounds good. I'll grab the bread and get us some bottled water."

"Do you want to drive?" Jill slapped turkey on the bread.

"No, they're just a block down the road. We can walk." Lexi tossed a piece of turkey into the kennel with the sheltie. "There you go, Lassie."

"I can't believe he got you that dog."

Lexi reached into the kennel and the dog licked her fingers. The puppies, four of them, curled around the momma, and they were growing fast. They were almost ready for Josie and Alyssa to spend time with them.

Lexi needed to write a note to remind herself to talk to the girls to see what they planned on doing to bring Josie and Silas together. And then she felt a little silly, because she was involving herself in the matchmaking attempts of two little girls. Did she really want to help stick sweet Josie Cane with Silas Marstow?

"Lexi?"

"I'm listening. The dog was sweet. Come on."

Jill opened the front door and Lexi followed her out, locking it behind them. She glanced in the direction of her burned-out home. Another dream undone.

She had other dreams. She could check into homes in Manhattan. Or she could start with the house on the east side of High Plains. Purely out of curiosity, she planned on making an appointment to see it. Maybe if she saw it she would have her answer. If she loved it and could buy it, she would stay. That sounded simple enough.

As they walked, she tried to think about life in Manhattan, and how different it would be. She wouldn't have these friends or her church.

She wouldn't have her patients or people like the Stalwarts.

"Earth to Lexi." Jill bumped her arm. "What's up?"

"I was thinking about how it would feel to leave here."

"I wish you wouldn't."

Lexi shrugged. "I know. Don't worry, I'm not going to make hasty decisions. Okay, I guess I am being a little crazy about this, but I promise I'll slow down and pray."

"I'm glad to hear that. I do think you should look at that house you like. Oh, and think about your friends."

"You're right, I have a great career and wonderful friends. But Manhattan isn't the other side of the world. We could still get together for lunch and to shop."

"At real stores?"

"As if our stores in High Plains aren't real," Lexi teased.

"Shall we go to the Bartons' house?" Jill pointed to a house a block away from where they were. Blue tarps still covered a vast section of roof. Lexi nodded her head. The entire town had been covered with blue tarps after the tornado. A quick fix for roofs that leaked, until someone could do the job of getting them fixed.

Most of the tarps were gone, now. But there were still a few people who couldn't afford the repairs and weren't getting government assistance. The blue tarps still covered sections of those roofs. All over town, churches were doing fundraisers to meet those needs.

High Plains Community Church had raised thousands of dollars at their carnival. And now the Garrisons' lumberyard was helping out with supplies. Lexi followed Jill to where Michael stood, a hammer in his hand and a perplexed look on his face.

"Problem?" Jill asked, smiling a little too big, a little too amused.

"I set my bag of nails down and now I can't find them."

Lexi pointed to his baseball cap, turned upside down on the bed of his truck. "Are those the nails, in your cap?"

He shook his head and laughed. "That's where I put them."

"Love does crazy things to a man," Lexi teased. "What can we do to help? With the building, I mean. Not with your relationship."

"Good question. I think the guys are looking for someone to help with the siding."

"Sounds like a job we can handle." Lexi pulled on leather work gloves that she'd stuffed into her pocket when they left the house. And Jill walked away, because she'd seen the man of her dreams.

"Lexi, Colt left town." Michael took the bag of nails out of his hat and dropped them into the tool belt he'd strapped around his waist. "Did he talk to you?"

"No." Her lungs caught, and she waited for the rest, because there had to be more. His eyes were narrowed and he looked down, staring at a spot on the ground for a full minute before looking up to make eye contact.

"He has a friend on the Wichita police force. I think he was going to visit him, maybe go fishing."

"He needs some time off."

"I'm worried that it's more than time off. He's mentioned in the past that his friend keeps trying to talk him into moving over there."

"He won't leave, Michael." Or would he? Not that it mattered to her. They were moving on. Maybe they were both going in new directions?

She leaned against the side of the truck and waited for the world to stop spinning. She had come to terms with the idea of her life without him in it. But she had planned it with him still in High Plains, close enough to touch.

This ached deep inside her, the way it had hurt two years ago when they'd finally called it quits.

"Lexi, don't give up."

She nodded and remembered that only moments earlier she'd been thinking about faith, and all of that peace she thought she had. Closing her eyes, she realized it was still there, still within grasp.

A prayer away.

She sighed and let out a deep breath. "I'm fine."

"Of course you are." Michael handed her a hammer. "And one thing to remember, Colt is praying. He came to me and asked me to pray with him."

"That's good. And really, maybe it's time for Colt and me to move on, to let go of the past."

Letting go didn't feel good. But it felt a lot like letting God have control, and she knew He wasn't surprised by any of this. As surely as He had taken care of Tommy, and Kasey, even Jesse Logan, as surely as He had planned a special friendship between Alyssa and Lilli, she knew He would take care of her. He would take care of Colt.

Colt flexed his fingers on the steering wheel because he'd been driving for hours. Somewhere along the way he'd changed directions. He'd been on the road, heading for Wichita, but he'd taken a different exit, a highway going north and then east. He was heading for Iowa, and Gavin's family.

He needed to know that they were okay.

For whatever reason, they held the key to his

own future. He didn't know how to explain that, so he hadn't told anyone. He had called his buddy in the Wichita police department and told him he couldn't make it, not this week. But he hadn't called home.

Lexi. He wanted to call her, to tell her he was thinking about her. He wouldn't. They hadn't spoken all week. By the time he got home, she might be gone, back to Manhattan.

If he let her go, she'd find someone else. She'd have a family. With someone else. And that was the right thing. Or so he'd been telling himself. She deserved security in the form of a husband who would come home every night, always be there for her and the kids they would have.

She would never get that knock on the door, telling her that her husband had been killed in the line of duty.

And as he thought through those ideas, he remembered Michael asking him where faith came into all of this. And Colt had known then that he couldn't continue to control his own life, not like this. He had spent a few years, quite a few, having faith in his own abilities. It had landed him here, on this road, divorced and living with the guilt of something he couldn't control.

So he was on his way to Iowa, because he had lived with guilt for three years and it was time to face Gavin's wife. He needed to know that she'd forgiven him.

And then he'd move on. Whatever that meant.

He drove faster, miles slipping away as he approached the little town in southwest Iowa where Lisa lived, with the three kids she'd had with Gavin. Three kids, left without a dad. A wife, left to carry on alone.

That had rocked his world a few years ago.

He had been consumed with guilt, for letting his fellow officer down. Michael's words came back, hitting hard, because it was the first time anyone had ever said them to him.

*Colt, are you keeping yourself from having what you want—Lexi and children—because you feel guilty? You didn't get to Gavin quick enough. You couldn't save him. You couldn't save his wife the pain of losing him. So you shut yourself off and you pushed aside your own happiness. Is it about protecting Lexi, or your own guilt, because you're alive and he isn't?*

When Michael first made that statement, Colt had walked out of their counseling session.

Small towns didn't have grief counselors for their officers. The week after Gavin had been shot, the state had sent a counselor, but Colt hadn't needed to talk. He really hadn't needed to tell someone what he felt about losing Gavin. He knew.

He might have known more if he'd talked to someone three years ago. If he had talked to Lexi. If he had shared with her instead of shutting himself off, things might have been different.

One hand on the steering wheel, he dialed his phone. Michael answered.

"You were right," Colt said. "I felt guilty. I should have been there sooner. I could have stopped it from happening. I could have been on that stretch of road, instead of Gavin."

"Hold on, I'm in the middle of hammering shingles on a roof. Let me get down so we can talk."

"Don't fall."

"I'm not planning on it." Michael grunted and exhaled, his breath loud through the phone. "Okay, where are you?"

"On my way to Iowa."

"I see. Why?"

"I have to see Gavin's wife. I have to tell her how sorry I am. I have to deal with what happened." He leaned forward, looking for his exit. "I have to do that so I can move on with my life."

"With Lexi."

"With Lexi. I can't live without her. I've tried for two years, and it hasn't been much like living. I think I could go on, I could survive without her, but I would miss her. Forever."

"You'd better hurry home before you lose her."

"I'll be back in a couple of days."

"I'll see you then." Hammering again, on Michael's end, and people talking in the background. They were working on homes.

"Could you do me a favor?" Colt turned off the highway.

Of course he would. Colt told Michael the plan and when he hung up, he felt pretty good. He felt better than he had in three years. His chest was lighter. The weight was lifting.

Three hours later he pulled up to a pretty house on a quiet street. It was dark, and there were lights on inside the house. Through the sheer curtains he could see a boy, tall and gangly, standing in the center of the room. A younger boy was jumping up and down, grabbing at something the older boy held over his head.

Colt smiled, knowing that game.

He got out of his car and walked up to the front door. He hadn't called. He should have. Two years was a long time. He didn't know what had happened in her life after she moved here.

He paused at the door, but it opened, not giving him the opportunity to walk away. The man standing in front of him was tall and broad-shouldered. Huge. Maybe it wasn't her house.

"I'm looking for Lisa…." He felt like a fifteen-year-old kid, palms sweating and feet itching to run.

"She's here. Could I ask who you are?"

"Colt Ridgeway. I'm the chief of police in High Plains, Kansas. Her husband worked for the county I live in."

And then she was there, smiling and looking as if life had been good to her—her brown hair had light streaks and her eyes sparkled with laughter because a baby, barely walking, held her fingers.

"Colt, what in the world…"

"I'm sorry, I should have called."

"No, that's not what I mean. I'm glad you're here, I just wondered why. This isn't really in your jurisdiction."

"I was driving." He sighed. "I was actually on my way to Wichita."

"You're nowhere near Wichita." She laughed, and the man standing next to her motioned him inside. He held out a hand.

"I'm Jake Barton. I'm Lisa's husband."

Husband. He hadn't known. Colt took the offered hand. "Good to meet you. I really don't want to intrude."

"You're not intruding," Lisa insisted. "Come in and have coffee. After a drive like that, you probably need some caffeine."

"Coffee would be good. I don't want to be any trouble."

"You're not."

He followed her through the house, seeing her kids, who were smiling and playing a game. The last time he'd seen them, a month after their dad's funeral, they'd still been quiet, still sad, still grieving the loss of their father. Lisa had been strong, telling him it wasn't his fault, he should let it go, and spend time with his wife.

But he hadn't spent time with Lexi, because he'd felt guilty for still having someone to come home to. He shook his head and followed Lisa and her husband into a big kitchen.

"Have a seat and tell me why you're here, Colt. I know you didn't get this far from home by accident."

He sat down at the island. "It wasn't really planned. I was going to meet a friend in Wichita, and I made a decision to come here and check on you. I had your address in my cell phone with your number. I should have called."

"You're fine." Lisa poured water into the coffeepot. "How's Lexi. Do you two have kids yet?"

He shook his head, unsure of what to say. Lisa set the coffeepot down and looked at him, her eyes narrowing as she got it.

"Colt, what's going on?"

"We're divorced. I wasn't a very good husband. I…"

"You couldn't let go of what happened." She switched the pot on and sat down next to him. Her new husband picked up the baby, touched her shoulder and then left the room. "Colt, look at me, I moved on. Gavin would have wanted us to move on. He wouldn't have wanted us to lose our joy in life. He wanted you and Lexi to have kids."

"I know, we talked about it. But when I knocked on your door that night and I saw what it did to you, to your kids…"

"You didn't want that to happen to Lexi."

"That, and now I realize that I didn't know how to have so much happiness when Gavin was gone. He wouldn't be coming back to his family."

"Gavin isn't in Heaven worrying about this, about you having your life with your wife. He would feel bad if he knew that you'd tossed it all away out of guilt."

"I'm starting to realize that." He folded his hands and stared down at the finger where he'd once worn a wedding band. "I feel like I've been on a long journey and I'm nearly home. I'm finding my way back to having faith. It's been a long time. I think I blamed God as much as I blamed myself."

He was seeing things from a different perspective. He was seeing Tommy with a family, and Michael reunited with Heather.

"You're not so unusual, Colt. We all deal with grief, with guilt, with blame." She covered his hand with her own. "We struggle with doubting God's presence. And in those moments, we dig down and look at all He's done. We use the tools He's given us to get through."

"Lisa, I really appreciate you inviting me in this way."

"Colt, you were one of Gavin's dearest friends. He wouldn't want to see you hurting like this. I don't want to see you like this, throwing away what means so much to you."

"Thank you."

"You're welcome."

"So, a lot has been going on in your life." From where he sat he could see her kids, the new husband and the baby.

"Oh, you wouldn't believe the half of it. We're getting ready to move to South America. We're going to be missionaries."

She got up and poured coffee. Colt took it and listened as she told how she'd met her husband, about the new baby girl and their move to South America.

And he kept thinking of Lexi, and what it would be like to have a child that looked like her.

## Chapter Fourteen

Lexi drove past the police station. Colt was on duty again. He was back from Wichita. And he hadn't called her. He hadn't stopped by to say hello.

What did that mean?

A block past the police station she saw Chico. The crazy dog was chasing someone's cat. Lexi pulled over and whistled. He looked at the cat, in the process of climbing a tree, and back to Lexi.

Master. Cat. Master. Cat. She laughed, because he was standing there with his tongue hanging out, his tail wagging and looking from her to the cat, and back again.

"Chico, now." The dog took a few steps in her direction, looking perfectly obedient, and then he dodged past her and headed for town, to Colt. That silly dog whistle.

What would Colt do with Chico in a city the size

of Wichita? If that was his plan, master and dog would both be miserable. She knew that, even if he didn't. But who was she to throw stones when she had driven into Manhattan twice in the last week to look at houses her mom had found for her.

Today she was giving herself a break and taking a look at the house in High Plains—her dream house.

She pulled up in front of the craftsman with the dark shingled siding. Jill had met her and was parked in the driveway. They were planning on peeking in the windows, to see if it was as cute as Lexi imagined. And then she planned on calling the Realtor.

Jill got out of her car and pointed to the sign. "Too late."

Lexi nodded and felt like crying, because something else had been taken. The words *Under Contract* now covered the real estate sign.

"It's just a silly house. That shouldn't upset me so much. You have to possess something for it to be taken away from you. A dream isn't a possession."

"It was a dream of yours for a long time. You've always loved this place." Jill gave her an easy hug. "Come on, maybe the contract will fall through."

Lexi laughed. "You want me to hope for someone else's misfortune?"

"No, not for misfortune, only that they come to

their senses and decide they would never want this house."

Colt's Jeep cruised past, Chico in the passenger seat, head out the window. Lexi waved, but he didn't stop. He barely looked her way.

"Well, now that's odd." Jill bit down on her bottom lip. "What's up with him?"

"I don't know. He came home from Wichita, went to work and I haven't heard from him."

"I thought the two of you were working things out?"

"We were trying to be friends. That was an obvious mistake. Now we can't even talk to each other." Because being together had been too big a reminder of what they'd lost.

Jill didn't say anything. Lexi shot her a look and Jill shrugged. "I'm not commenting. No matter what I say, you're going to do what you're going to do."

"I guess you're right."

"So, you don't want my advice?"

Lexi unlocked her truck and got in. "Not really. Besides, I think this house being under contract is my answer. I was holding out for this place. With it taken off the table, I'm going to give serious consideration to the house in Manhattan."

"I think…"

Jill backed away for Lexi to close the truck door. Lexi's phone buzzed.

"Shoot, the Johnstons, they have a mare down. I guess you'll have to tell me what you think later."

"Nice save..." Jill hesitated. "I have a date tonight."

"Someone to spend your weekends with other than me!"

"Sorry, sweetie. Lunch tomorrow?"

"Lunch." Lexi started her truck. "I'll see you then."

"Lex, don't give up."

"I'm not giving up. I'm exploring new plans for my life."

A few hours later Lexi pulled into her drive, exhausted and ready for something to eat, even if it was just a sandwich. She didn't care what it was, as long as she could eat it sitting on her couch and vegging in front of her TV. Something moved at the corner of her house, catching her attention.

Chico. He walked to the front door and sat down. Lexi climbed out of her truck and walked toward the dog, who didn't move. Her heart caught a little, because that wasn't normal for Chico.

"What's up, buddy?"

Chico's tail thumped the ground and he lay down, whining a little.

Lexi kneeled in front of him, rubbing his soft

head. The dog leaned into her, whining. "I guess you can't tell me what's wrong."

She put a hand under his head and tilted it to look into eyes that were clear. He licked her hand and crawled closer. Something hung on his collar. Lexi moved the leather strap and pulled off the piece of paper tied to the rabies tag with string.

A phone number. She dialed and waited.

"Hello, Miss Harmon, how are you today." Colt smiled and he couldn't begin to explain to anyone how that moment and hearing her voice on the other end of the line felt.

"Colt, what have you done to our dog?"

"I told him to stay. Amazing, huh?"

"Yes, amazing. But he's your dog."

"He still loves you." He still loved her. And he could say it now. He wasn't afraid. He wanted her to know that.

"That's good." A wistful tone to her voice vibrated through him. He wanted to end it all now, but he couldn't.

"I need to talk to you."

"We're talking…" She hesitated. "This is starting to feel like police harassment."

"I'd rather think of it as a friendly hello."

"Fine, hello. Did you have a nice trip?" Miffed. He knew that tone. He wanted to remind her of another time they'd played this game, a scavenger hunt. She'd found tickets to a vacation at the end of the game.

This time he had to go a little easier on her.

"I did have a good trip. I'm sorry I haven't called. I had a lot to take care of. And I noticed you have a Realtor sign in your front yard. Going somewhere?"

"Manhattan. Could you please tell me what this is all about? I'm really hungry, and I'm tired."

"Okay, but you have to humor me."

"Humor you, how?"

Man, he really loved her. She was smart and beautiful and loving. She made him want to start having a family tomorrow. Or as soon as they could say "I do" again. If she would have him.

"There's a note under the doormat."

"Fine." She paused. "I have to find a house with a blue roof and hardy mums the color of a sunset. Do you know that describes every house in this neighborhood?"

"It has a blue door."

"Okay, blue door. And what will people think when I walk up and pull something off the windshield of their car?"

"They won't mind."

Because everyone in town, but her, knew what he was up to. He knew people would be watching out windows and from backyards, waiting. Because Tommy had a family. Michael and Heather had found each other again. And now Colt and Lexi were making up.

One tornado, a lot of damage, and lives restored. He couldn't fix it all in his mind, but he could see that God had used that storm to bring him to this place, where he had faith, and where he could look beyond the bad things that happened and see God using it for good.

He would tell her that later. When they met face-to-face.

He would tell her that God doesn't stop every bad thing from happening, but He protects and He restores. He redeems.

God even redeems and protects stubborn, hard-headed cops who think they have to take care of everyone because they believe God is falling down on the job.

He shook his head at his own foolishness.

"Colt, what are we doing?"

"Playing a game." He heard her sigh. "See you in about thirty minutes. If you're that good."

"Um-hmm, you'd better have a steak dinner on the other end of this little game."

He hung up. And for a moment he watched, because he could see her walk to the corner of her yard. She stood there, the breeze lifting that brown silk curtain of hair.

He had never known anyone like her. And she hadn't given up on him.

Lexi walked down the block in the direction the note told her to go. Colt was out there somewhere, she knew he was. She didn't see him, but he was watching; she could tell by the change in Chico, suddenly on the alert, his ears up and tail wagging. That was the dog's "Colt's here" look.

For a moment back there, she'd been upset with him. She was tired. He hadn't stopped by all week. Now he wanted to play a game. There were reasons to be mad. And reasons to feel some funny sense of hope, because Colt sounded like Colt again. He sounded like the man she had married, a man who found humor and joy in simple things. Like a scavenger hunt.

As she passed a house with children, she stopped and looked. A blue door. A paper, held to the windshield of the family minivan by the wiper blades, flapped in the breeze. A little girl waved, as if Lexi had been expected.

She picked up the paper and read it, feeling fourteen and a little silly. "There's a piece to this puzzle at a house with red shutters."

That was it, red shutters. And how did she know

what to look for when she found the house? She started walking, looking, feeling ridiculous. When she caught up with him, she was going to let him know how she felt.

How she felt. Like the fact that she still loved him. Maybe they were back to square one, still not communicating effectively. He couldn't know how she felt, because she hadn't told him.

She picked up her steps, in a hurry now to get to him, to see what he would say. And then hesitating, because what if he told her they couldn't go back? Friendship hadn't worked and marriage hadn't worked. Then what?

The house with the red shutters was easy to find. An elderly woman walked down the drive and handed Lexi a large envelope. She took it and thanked the woman, who smiled big and walked back to her house.

A note was attached. This was getting crazy. If he wanted her to go somewhere, he could have just driven her. She pulled her cell phone out of her pocket and dialed his number, the real one, not the disposable number he'd given her to start the game.

His voice mail picked up. "This is Colt. Lexi, if you have the package, keep walking straight and take your next left. There's a bottle of water at a nearby house, because this is a long walk. And stop frowning."

She stomped on, feeling sillier by the minute. A man mowing his lawn stopped mowing. He waved her toward him. When she approached, he held out the bottle of water. His smile was crooked and he laughed a little.

"You could tell me what's going on. It seems everyone in town knows." She unscrewed the top from the bottle and took a drink.

"A few of us know, but we kind of like surprises and well, we like you and Colt."

"So, was there some kind of meeting that took place and you all decided to have this little scavenger hunt?"

"It did sort of start out at the last town council meeting…"

She laughed then, because she could picture them all at a meeting, talking about the new storm siren, her pets and then this. Whatever this was. But she had a feeling the mayor had something to do with it. Maybe they were finally building an animal shelter!

"How much farther?" She handed him the empty water bottle.

"Two blocks. Not that far." He pointed. "And then go left."

Out of town. She sighed. At least she was wearing comfortable shoes.

As she walked, she forgot to be upset with Colt

for playing games. It was a pretty evening, close to October, and some of the leaves were changing colors. Families were in their yards, enjoying the good weather, and dogs barked as kids played.

She loved it here. She had dreamed of this life as a child, wanting a place like this to call home. She had wanted kids that played together in a backyard while she and Colt cooked burgers on the grill.

For a while it had looked possible.

"Lexi." His voice, calling her name. She looked up, remembering where she was and what she was supposed to be doing. She had gotten lost in thought. But there was Colt, standing in the road, next to the real estate sign of the house she loved. And now, rather than Under Contract, the sign said Sold.

Her heart thumped hard in her chest.

Colt was waiting in that yard. For her.

"I love this house." She smiled, but it wavered and her eyes filled with tears. "Did you buy it?"

"I did. Come on up." He slipped an arm through hers and led her up the brick sidewalk, up the steps to the wide front porch where petunias were still blooming in pots and mums were bright yellow and orange. The heavy scent of petunias perfumed the evening air that had suddenly gone still.

Colt pointed to a wicker seat; on the table next to it were scissors and a big glass of iced tea. And a sandwich.

"You brought food?"

"I knew you'd be hungry."

She wasn't hungry now. She had a bad case of butterflies.

"Colt, this has been fun." But not. "Please, let's stop now."

Because she couldn't take it anymore.

"Lexi, I've been through a lot in the last few years. We both have. We've been through more in the last two months. But I think we've also learned a lot."

"Yes, we have."

"I've learned things about myself that I didn't know."

"Okay." She smiled a little. "I could have told you, though."

"I think you tried, but there were things you didn't know. There were things that I think I knew, but I didn't deal with."

She pulled out a stool at the bar. "I'm listening."

"I didn't have faith." Tall and strong, he leaned against the rail of the porch, his face so boyish and sweet she wanted to hold him. "I was angry with God for what happened to my family, and then Gavin. The storm took me over the edge. When I saw people praying, I couldn't help but wonder where God was in the storm."

"Right here, with all of us, getting us through."

"I know that now. I know now that sometimes things happen that seem beyond anyone's control, but God isn't surprised, and He does have a plan. We have to trust Him."

"I'm glad, Colt, really so happy for you that you've found a way to have faith." But inside her heart was quaking, a mixture of fear and anticipation.

"Lexi, I shut you out because I was afraid. But also because of guilt. I let my fellow officer down. His wife and kids had to go on alone, and I could go home to you every night."

"You stopped coming home to me, Colt. You slept at the station, or on the couch. I spent my childhood with that scenario, alone, with my parents off doing their job. I didn't want it to be my marriage. I still don't."

"I know." He stepped back, motioning her down the stairs of the porch. "I let you down. And I don't want to let you down again. I don't want to lose you, or the dreams we had."

"We dreamed of having a family," she whispered, stepping closer, following him off the porch.

He leaned forward, capturing her lips in a soft kiss, opening her to him in a way that hadn't happened in so long. The kiss promised something wonderful in the future. He whispered that he loved her and kissed her again, holding her close, cupping her cheeks with hands that were strong.

The kiss ended and he held her close. He moved, but still held her. "Lexi, I love you," he whispered into her hair. "I know I've said the words, but I plan on proving it. But what I don't know is if you still love me."

She rested her forehead on his shoulder and nodded, because words wouldn't come and tears were cascading down her cheeks, because their dream hadn't ended. And Colt loved her.

Weeks of rebuilding a friendship had changed everything.

"I love you." She finally said the words and he held her tight, as if he might never let her go.

"I have something for you." He backed away, releasing her.

When she turned, he released a cord and a sign fell from the overhang of the porch.

Lexi, Marry Me. Red letters on white, hanging across the front of the porch.

The house she had wanted. She turned back to Colt. He handed her the envelope she'd picked up along the way.

"Open it."

She did. She slid out the papers, recognizing their divorce papers. New tears trickled down her cheeks as he handed her scissors that were sitting on the post of the porch rail. She took them with hands that trembled and sliced through the papers.

"Lexi Ridgeway, will you marry me, soon? Will you have my children and live in this house with me, forever?" He dug around in his pocket, for a minute looking panicked. "And forgive me for ruining the most romantic thing I've ever done in my life, because I have something that I almost forgot."

Lexi laughed a little and wiped at the tears.

Colt had something in his hand and he kneeled down in front of her, taking her left hand. Lexi sobbed because when he looked up, he had tears in his eyes and her wedding ring in his hand.

"Lexi, forgive me for keeping these from you. But I had a feeling I might need them again. I hoped. The minister who married us said that these rings stand for eternity. And I believe they do. And I believe God has a plan for our lives together. I found these rings, Lexi, your rings, after I prayed for God to show me what to do. It was the first real prayer I had prayed in years, and God heard."

"Colt."

"Marry me again."

He was still on one knee and Lexi wanted to be close to him. She dropped to her knees in front of him and reached to pull him close.

"I'll marry you." She brushed her cheek

against his, smiling. "You could have asked me this at my house."

"I wanted this proposal to be one you'd never forget."

She closed her eyes as he kissed her again. And she would never forget what God had done in their lives, or what it meant to believe in forever with a man she loved.

\* \* \* \* \*

Dear Reader,

*Rekindled Hearts* was an opportunity given to me by the editors of Love Inspired®, and I so appreciate this chance to write a story about people surviving. Not only did the citizens of High Plains survive the devastation of the tornado, they came together and they found a faith that was stronger than ever.

Colt and Lexi are like so many of us—they faced challenges in their marriage brought on by fear, lack of communication and even lack of trust. When it got too difficult, they walked away from each other and from the love that had brought them together. This book brings them back together, but it takes work, it takes communication. They have to face the problems that broke down the marriage to begin with, before they can start to put it back together. In the end, they do find that their love is strong enough, and so is their faith—in God and in each other.

In the midst of life's storms, God brings beauty. From tragedy, He brings joy. What looked like the worst possible thing for a small town became the catalyst for many good things to happen in the lives of the citizens of High Plains.

*Brenda Minton*

# QUESTIONS FOR DISCUSSION

1. As the tornado roars toward High Plains, Kansas, Police Chief Colt Ridgeway is patrolling the town, but also thinking about the safety of his ex-wife. God also crosses his mind, as does the thought that he isn't ready to die. Why do you think all of those thoughts are rolling through his mind? What type of person is he?

2. Lexi is worried about her ex-husband, Colt. She knows she should be in the basement, but she's torn by worry. How would you react in her situation, with someone you care about possibly in danger, and knowing that you yourself could be in danger?

3. The tornado was not something that could be controlled, and afterward, it was time to rebuild. But even in rebuilding, there is much that is out of a person's control. In the first chapter Lexi knows that the town will never be the same, even after it is rebuilt. Why does she feel that way?

4. How discouraged would the citizens be at

this point, with so much still ahead of them even weeks later? How would you feel if you were in their shoes?

5. Colt notices that people return to church because of the tornado. Why are churches full after something like a tornado or national tragedy? What happens to those people as months go by?

6. Lexi, like so many of us, has dreams of what she thinks a perfect life would be. She knows that life is never perfect, but do you think those dreams affected her marriage?

7. Lexi knows that perfect doesn't exist. What do you think she really wanted from life, her marriage and her faith?

8. If we're looking to change our lives, how does it help us to look at someone else as an example, the way Lexi looked to her neighbors when she was growing up? How can that hurt us?

9. Colt is controlled by a sense of obligation to people and a desire to keep everyone safe. How does his faith, or lack of faith, affect that trait?

10. The tornado, Marie Logan's death, the loss of Tommy's dog and the loss of homes are a few of the bad things that happened in High Plains. What is the normal reaction when these types of things happen to us? How can we see God moving, in the book and in our lives, if we look beyond what we see as a bad situation?

11. Lexi wants to fix her failed marriage, but fear keeps her from giving in completely. What do you think causes her fear?

12. Colt begins to see God at work in the lives of the people of High Plains. How does that change his relationship with Lexi, and how does it give him faith?

13. Would their marriage have been stronger if they had communicated more effectively? Colt's neighbor told him that he needed to do more than listen; he needed to hear what Lexi was telling him. What did the neighbor mean by that?

14. Colt and Lexi plan to marry again. Life isn't perfect. No marriage is perfect. What makes a relationship work?

15. When Jill and Lexi discuss marriage, they talk about trading one problem for another. What did they realize as they were discussing marriage?

*Turn the page for a sneak preview
of the next heartwarming*
AFTER THE STORM *book,*
*THE MATCHMAKING PACT*
*by Carolyne Aarsen.*
*Available in October 2009
from Steeple Hill Books.*

Above the sound of emergency sirens approaching, Josie heard her niece calling her name. Josie hugged herself, praying frantically as Silas Marstow carefully made his way over the downed power line, then through the debris on the lawn to the back of the house. The tornado had devastated their quiet, peaceful town. *Please Lord, let those girls be safe.*

After what seemed like an eternity, Silas came from behind the house, his daughter on his hip, his other hand holding Alyssa's.

Alyssa was carrying a plastic bag, but Josie was too relieved to pay it much attention.

She ran toward Alyssa and swept her into her arms.

"You silly girl. I was so worried." She dropped to her knees, her hands slipping over Alyssa's dear face. "Are you okay? What were you thinking leaving like that?"

Alyssa glanced at Silas's daughter, Lilli, then

back at Josie. "I wanted to get something. From the house. For Lilli."

Fear and anger fought for dominance, but relief took the upper hand.

"Why didn't you ask me? Why did you go without telling me? Do you know what just happened?"

Alyssa looked around and sighed. "The storm left a big mess."

Her simple, matter-of-fact statement released some of Josie's tension.

"It was very dangerous to go to the house without telling me." Josie's voice trembled.

"I'm sorry. But now I have my present for Lilli. I had it ready in the kitchen but forgot it." She glanced up at Silas. "Are we going to the church? I want to wrap it there. I have some pretty paper."

Silas shifted his daughter on his hip, his tanned forearms holding her close as he shot a frown toward Josie. "No. I'm taking Lilli home. Now."

"Happy birthday, Lilli," Alyssa said with a wide smile.

Josie saw Silas's face go blank, then he closed his eyes and pulled his lower lip between his teeth.

And she knew the single father had forgotten his only daughter's birthday.

"Thanks, Alyssa," Lilli said with a huge grin, seemingly unaware of her father's mistake. Then she turned to Silas. "Can Alyssa and Miss Josie come over for a party for my birthday?"

Silas shot a glance over his shoulder at the remains of Josie's house, something she'd been avoiding doing ever since they turned down this street.

"I think Miss Cane has other things on her mind right now." Silas put Lilli down, but clung to her hand. He looked around the street as one of the emergency crews ran to the house beside Josie's and another to hers.

Josie turned away, unable to look at the wreckage any longer. Later she could absorb it. Later she could figure out what had to happen. For now, she had to find out what had happened to her grandmother.

"We gotta get going," Silas said, shoving his hand through his hair, as if unsure what to do. "Glad that you and the girls are okay." He gave her a tight smile, then walked down the littered street, leading his daughter by the hand.

Josie watched him go as a hard shivering seized her body.

Aftershock, she reasoned, hugging herself. She tried to keep her thoughts at bay, tried to corral them into a corner.

But they buzzed past her defenses. Was her grandmother okay? Who else could have been hurt?

"I have to go find Gramma," Josie said suddenly.

"Do you think she's okay?"

"We'll find out." She was about to leave when a fireman called her back.

"Ma'am. We have to ask you to head back to the church." He walked over to her, full of purpose and determination. "We're sending everyone there for now."

"But my grandmother…"

"We'll be giving out news as we find things out. It's too dangerous to go wandering the streets on your own. Gas leaks, lines down. Sorry."

Josie hugged herself again, glancing over her shoulder in the direction of her grandmother's home.

This storm had changed everything. It had blasted into town, torn up homes and, even though it had happened only half an hour ago, Josie knew it had completely rearranged her life and her plans.

Guess she wouldn't be moving away from High Plains this fall after all.

*Two days later*

"So what are you going to do, Lilli?" Alyssa pressed her mouth close to her aunt's cell phone, hoping she hadn't noticed that it and Alyssa were missing from the classroom in the church. If her aunt knew Alyssa was using her cell phone, and why, she would be mad. "If you're not allowed to come to the after-school program anymore, how are my aunt and your dad going to fall in love like we planned?"

"We need to make a pact."

"Is that a sin?"

"No, silly." Lilli laughed. "It's a promise that you and I are going to make sure that my dad and your aunt are going to fall in love."

"A matchmaking pact."

"Yeah. A pact."

"But we have to hurry because my aunt still says we're going to move away. And if we move, they're never going to fall in love." Alyssa looked back over her shoulder, but no one was in the hallway. "So we're going to make a pact and make a plan."

"Right. And this is what we'll do."

Alyssa listened carefully, and as Lilli told her the plan, she started to smile. This might work really good. And if it did, she would have a dad again.

And Lilli would get another mom.

# *Love Inspired®*
# SUSPENSE
## RIVETING INSPIRATIONAL ROMANCE

These contemporary tales
of intrigue and romance
feature Christian characters
facing challenges to their faith...
and their lives!

**Four new Love Inspired Suspense titles are
available every month wherever books are
sold, including most bookstores, supermarkets,
drug stores and discount stores.**

Steeple
Hill®

Visit:
**www.steeplehillbooks.com**